DAPHNE

by

R B Koester

Bronze Press

Published by Bronze Press, LLC
www.bronzepress.com

Library of Congress Control Number: 2024917745
ISBN: 979-8-218-49585-5
eBook ISBN: 979-8-9914155-0-7

Cover design and illustration by Pawan Anjana

Acknowledgments

I would like to thank, Anthony Mangano for his insights and support as my invaluable writing coach and editor, Maya Myers for her honest and thoughtful reviews and assistance with editing three of my novels, Sam Wright for proofreading assistance, and of course my family for encouraging my writing.

To Jen

DAPHNE

Part I

1. On the Way to Mieza—343 BCE

Kallos looked up at one of the tall mountains northern Macedonia was known for as he steered his new chariot ahead with breakneck speed. Two black stallions hurtled forward, testing its strength. The chariot's large wheels and newly crafted steel axle allowed for tight turns. It was not a comfortable ride, but Kallos did not care. He was far more concerned about appearance than comfort. Tall and muscular with curly blond hair, he was the epitome of athletic form, and he knew it.

No one but the gods was watching him on the remote country road, but Kallos stood tall nevertheless, reveling in the racing victory he'd just achieved at the pan-Macedonian festival in Pieria. He'd become an instant hero, a change in status he needed. His background alone was not enough to get him where he was going.

He was on his way to Mieza, where the future leaders of Macedonia—including Alexander, the son of King Philip— would gather to be educated by none other than the well-respected scholar Aristoteles. Recently rejected as the new leader of Plato's school in Athens, Aristoteles was in need of employment, and at any rate could not refuse the king's demands. King Philip thought it important for his thirteen-year-old son to experience life beyond the constant tutelage of his mother. The king knew the importance of restraint and control in human relationships, and he believed that only outside his mother's influence would Alexander become a man who knew what he wanted on his own.

King Philip had even given up some of his own control over Alexander: he'd arranged the boy's schooling far away from the palace, but hand-picked the teacher. Aristoteles's father was King Philip's physician, and Philip had taken an interest in Aristoteles even when he was still a child. The king told Aristoteles that he could design the curriculum, so long as some form of athleticism was part of it. And, the king declared, there must be a chariot race between Kallos and Alexander. It was an unusual request, and Aristoteles did not understand the motivation behind it, but it was not his place to question the king.

The gods smiled approvingly at Kallos's pride. One of their own—Apollo, god of sports, arts, healing, and knowledge—would be competing in Mieza. They did not know which of the participants Apollo would choose to disguise himself as. He had kept that a secret. As they watched, many of them suspected that Kallos might actually be Apollo, who was after all the god who was believed by humans to ride a chariot across the sky that carried the sun. With his curly blond hair, Kallos racing across the countryside bore a certain resemblance.

The gods were happy to watch another drama unfold. Even Zeus, the god of gods, and his wife Hera were watching. Hera kept her enthusiasm hidden and, feeling it was beneath them to get too caught up, urged Zeus to do the same. Zeus complied. Apollo was his son, but Hera was not his mother, Leda was. Zeus knew he had to be careful around Hera when it came to Apollo, so he had kept a distance from the boy even though he desperately longed for a more meaningful relationship with his son.

For his part, Apollo was going to Mieza not to be schooled, but to find Daphne, his first love. Some time ago, Eros, the god of love, had become jealous of Apollo's skill at archery. Eros shot Apollo with a golden arrow, which made Apollo fall madly in love with Daphne. Eros then shot Daphne with a lead arrow, making her indifferent to Apollo. It was terribly cruel act of mischief. Apollo could not resist constant pursuit of Daphne, while Daphne remained perpetually resistant.

After much back and forth, Daphne's father, Peneus, a river god, put an end to the ordeal by turning Daphne into a laurel tree. The loss was devastating for Apollo. He longed for Daphne yet had no choice but to move on. He pursued many other relationships, possibly too many, always in search of what he'd felt for Daphne, but none ever compared to the woman who had opened his heart. She was special, and he wanted her back.

Eventually Daphne had grown tired of her passive existence as a tree, feeling it an unfair confinement. All she could do was observe a small place in the forest from a safe distance. Daphne wanted an active life, one in which she could make choices, react to situations, and roam the way she had before. This desire grew over time, to the point that she craved drama—any drama, good or bad. Yet Daphne knew that her father was pleased with the safety this existence offered her and would not allow her return to her former life.

When Daphne heard that Aristoteles was going to teach in Mieza, she thought it was just the kind of opportunity she might persuade her father to let her experience. What could go wrong studying in a remote school with Aristoteles? This was no potentially treacherous life in a city; it was simply a chance to study at a school in the countryside.

Peneus was reluctant at first, wary of the risk for renewed misery. He was sure that Daphne did not have enough experience to know how to handle herself. Still, Daphne insisted, until finally Peneus decided it was better to allow her to explore than to let her stew over speculation about a better life. He turned Daphne into a human and a boy, so she could participate in classes. Daphne chose the name Perseus. Peneus did not know that the gods were watching when he effected the transformation, so he had no inkling that Apollo might renew his pursuit.

Daphne, as Perseus, was riding a solitary horse at a measured speed toward Mieza at the same time that Kallos was hurtling in his chariot toward the town. Perseus was savoring every part of the trip, not in a rush, happy to have escaped the confinement of the tree—appreciating the fields of wildflowers far in the distance, enjoying the warm afternoon wind, and noticing new sounds and smells. It was wonderful to move! To be immersed in changing scenery, to make small decisions like where to move the horse on the path.

Perseus was having fun, but it was still strange being in the mind of a human. What was this feeling of inadequacy and wanting? Why, Perseus wondered, was it all of a sudden so important to prove oneself? The feeling of wanting to learn under Aristoteles had shifted to wanting to also impress and be respected—but why?

Being in a human body felt strange, too. The only physical resemblance Perseus had to Daphne were soft green eyes and a long neck that on a boy made for broad shoulders as opposed to an elegant head. Perseus wanted to be attractive.

Peneus had assured Perseus that with an average but slightly muscular, thin build, curly black hair, and a face with some feminine qualities, Perseus would fit in. Perseus was not so sure.

Lost in thought, Perseus slumped on the horse, then quickly sat up straight. "I need to be a strong human," Perseus said out loud, as if saying it would make it so. "I will succeed in Mieza and be one of the best students. That should be enough. That is why I came, and that is what I shall do."

Krasi, another pupil, was not yet traveling. He lay in bed next to his latest conquest, a girl whose name he was trying to remember. Krasi lacked the ambition of Perseus. He was the son of a rich timber merchant who spoiled him, not because he loved Krasi, but because he was proud that he could provide his son the upbringing he did not have. It was a matter of pride, not love, and Krasi knew it.

Krasi's father had been ruthless and single-minded in his pursuit of wealth, often resorting to crime and threatening landowners who did not want to sell to him. While this approach may have been effective for the father's ends, the fear it instilled in people made it impossible for Krasi to build his own future, so Krasi had stopped trying. Instead, he lived in the moment—and fought his father wherever he could. When his father asked him to make friends with the sons of influential families, he refused. When his father asked him to court or at least compromise the daughters of wealthy landowners who could not be threatened otherwise, he refused. The only reason he'd agreed to come to Mieza was to get away—away from his father's obsessive pursuit of wealth.

Krasi's wavy, dark hair was seldom cut or combed, but he had an interesting triangular face, and his charm and constant smile made up for his average looks. He had learned that confidence and a relaxed manner could get him a lot of what he wanted, at least in relationships.

Zeus, who had frequently been unfaithful to his own wife Hera—the god of marriage, women, and family—looked down on Krasi as he struggled to remember the name of the girl he had slept with. Zeus could sympathize.

The marble throne where Zeus sat next to Hera was brilliantly white, and surrounded by an equally brilliant white temple. The marble rim of the nearby fire pit had been raised to ensure that the fire could not be seen. Ever since Prometheus had stolen fire for humans, Zeus could not stand to look upon it. It reminded him of disloyalty. Hera hated it, too, because fire was now common. If humans had it, she thought, the gods should not be seen with it.

Yet Zeus and Hera enjoyed watching humans. And at this moment, Zeus was particularly amused by the thought that Apollo might have chosen Krasi as his disguise, as a way to have some fun while pursuing Daphne.

In his old age, Zeus believed that brief encounters of the sort Krasi favored were acceptable. His main concern was that they created a habit—one Zeus had found hard to break. There was also the tedious fact that relationships with humans were unavoidably accompanied by emotions. Krasi—if he was indeed Apollo—had not recommitted to Daphne, but Daphne aside, he could be hurting the girl he was with.

Krasi eventually got up and, without washing, left the room at the inn where he was staying. He would get dirty on the ride anyway, he thought, and did not want to wake up the girl he'd slept with and go through the usual goodbyes with the awkward pretense that they might see one another again. It was the best for both of them, he thought, since surely neither considered the night's activities more than an infatuation.

A cowardly move, Zeus thought, just leaving like that. There was no shame in what Krasi had done, so he should have had the decency to say goodbye. Zeus would have admitted to not remembering the girl's name and would not have pretended that he would see her again. Krasi, however, appeared to be experiencing some self-doubt or regret, and it made him weak. To Zeus, this was a sign that Krasi was not ready for the encounters he was pursuing; perhaps he needed to develop a stronger sense of self before he undertook such distractions.

Krasi did not look at the innkeeper as he paid for the night. The innkeeper charged him extra, certainly too much for the filthy room he had given Krasi. The innkeeper should not have allowed Krasi, who was but fifteen, to stay there at all; he suspected Krasi would know this and would thus not make a fuss about the price.

Krasi turned one of the new uniform coins of the Macedonian kingdom in his hand. The coins were the same whether minted in Pella or Amphipoles, uniting the ever-expanding empire. King Philip had great ambitions for the empire, and he was succeeding. His armies had conquered and united Macedonia—most recently northern Macedonia, where Mieza was—and he was not going to stop there. The larger the empire became, the more it posed a threat to others, and the more important it became to increase its power. It was a task Alexander was to inherit. Growth was the only option, and a unifying currency was part of that.

Krasi reluctantly placed the beautiful tiny coin on the counter, marveling at the head of Apollo on the obverse. He could only admire it briefly before the innkeeper tucked it into his pocket. Krasi shrugged. If it were not for the beauty of the coin, he could not have cared less. His father was paying him an enormous allowance, in hopes that Krasi would impress and befriend his fellow students—Alexander, in particular. Krasi's father was convinced this could be used to his advantage at some point; it never was a bad idea to befriend a future ruler. Krasi himself, however, cared neither for money nor connections—in fact, the further he could distance himself from these concerns of his father, the better.

The most aristocratic of the students besides Alexander was Phaenon. He came not from Pella or Athens but from a part of southern Macedonia, where his father was the lord of the region. Phaenon rode an exceedingly strong and beautiful brown stallion, a present from his father, who wanted not only to allow his son to show well in front of the other students, but to impress a potential bride.

Phaenon was over twenty, the oldest of the students, and still not married. He was tall, with unusually straight, shiny black hair and a strong set of teeth, but nothing else stood out. His looks, however, were not the reason he remained unwed. He had rejected all potential engagements suggested by his parents, most recently to the daughter of a general in King Philip's army, an overbearing and powerful man. Phaenon thought that the general's daughter had learned to be too deferential and obedient. While she was one of the nicest girls he had met, he felt that as a wife, she would be too timid to help him build a future. Phaenon told his mother he did not want a wife that would comfort him, but one who would be a partner in what he wanted to achieve.

Phaenon had not told his parents that he also felt none of the women they had introduced him to came from a powerful enough family. Phaenon was determined to use his marriage as a tool for advancement. He wanted to be rich, yes, but only because wealth led to power. Influence and the ability to make people do what he wanted—that was currency to Phaenon.

Phaenon's parents had arranged his schooling in Mieza in part for their son to meet yet another potential bride—Leviat, who by all accounts had a mind of her own. "Let's see how he does when he meets his equal," Phaenon's father said to his wife when the meeting was arranged.

Phaenon was inclined toward the potential match mostly because Leviat was daughter to the governor of the most recently conquered area of Macedonia. Phaenon saw Leviat as his best prospect yet.

"Who would name their daughter Leviat?" Phaenon said out loud, as he reluctantly rode his impressive stallion toward Mieza. Levithan was the name of a powerful sea snake that spread chaos and evil; though Phaenon was sure that was not why Leviat's parents had named her so, it entertained him to play with Leviat's name in his overeducated mind, already demeaning her. It was envy that powered his unkindness: Leviat already had the status and wealth that Phaenon had to marry for.

Phaenon's simple clothes made him look like a stable boy riding his master's impressive horse. He'd worked hard to further his family's businesses, and the pressure had been great. He saw his time in Mieza as an opportunity for temporary reprieve and dressed the part. He also did not mind keeping his ambition to himself.

Hera, watching Phaenon, appreciated his focus on success. "He will be faithful to his wife," she thought, "because he doesn't let his passions carry him away."

Hera thought about the qualities Apollo might choose in a human to best appeal to Daphne. After her imprisonment in a tree, would she seek the physical pleasures that were once again possible? Would she live in the moment or look to build a future? Daphne had been Apollo's first love, and Hera wondered what, if anything, he had learned from his many interludes since then. Would he cater to what Daphne was likely to want?

"Let him succeed only if he has shown the wisdom to know what Daphne is seeking," Hera said frostily.

Enduring Zeus's many indiscretions had demolished Hera's self-respect such that she now cared only about one thing —the proprieties of her position. It made her cold and aloof, an attitude Zeus had come to hate.

Zeus had learned to cater to reluctant women and commiserated with what lay ahead for Apollo. He recalled the considerable effort it had taken to seduce Leda, Apollo's mother. Zeus had turned himself into a swan, and at the end had become forceful. He was not proud of this.

"You overcomplicate this," Zeus said to Hera in frustration, wishing he had not thought about Leda. "Apollo knows what he is doing, and Daphne—sorry, *Perseus* may not be inclined to choose anyone."

Zeus worried that the lead arrow might still rule Daphne's heart. Had Apollo taken that into account?

"You overestimate the ability of men to be rational about these matters," Hera retorted.

Zeus ignored the jab. Hera often made such comments. She did not forgive his indiscretions.

The one person who could not be accused of overestimating the boys was Aristoteles, who strolled down a path near the grotto outside Mieza with Theophrastus, his deputy who'd come with him from Athens.

"Youth have exalted notions, because they have not been humbled by life or learned the necessary limitations," Aristoteles said to Theophrastus.

Though Theophrastus had studied with Aristoteles under Plato and was well versed in philosophy, he was a botanist at heart. He even looked the part with his big beard and the ever-present dirt on his clothes, on his hands, and under his fingernails. Theophrastus kept his hair long until it got in the way and his beard wild so he would have something to play with while analyzing his plants.

Theophrastus agreed with what Aristoteles was saying and did not feel a need to respond, though Aristoteles would have welcomed it. Aristoteles had chosen Theophrastus as his main assistant because he was smart and students listened to him. Despite his mild manner, Theophrastus had a thunderous voice that projected confidence even in areas that Aristoteles was unsure about.

"Their hopeful disposition makes them think themselves equal to great things," Aristoteles continued. "They would rather do noble things than useful things. I should play on that. We must start with what they aspire to."

Aristoteles looked at Theophrastus who was preoccupied by his new surroundings, by the forests descending from the mountains. The colder and wetter climate at Mieza's high altitude gave rise to a more diverse and abundant flora than what he'd been able to study in the arid lands around Athens. Theophrastus had long since discovered that water was a key nutrient for plants, and Mieza had proven this in a grandiose way.

Theophrastus finally looked up. "They aspire to be virtuous leaders," he responded knowing that Aristoteles expected a response. "We can discuss virtues, but you become a virtuous leader by developing good habits," Aristoteles said, "not through lectures."

2. Daphne and Apollo

When Apollo and Daphne met for the first time, before Daphne
was turned into a laurel tree, Daphne was a free spirit. She was
beautiful but did not care about her appearance. She kept her hair
loose, wore animal skins, and even had a distaste for beautiful
clothes and garlands. She did not care about being wanted, or
attracting potential suitors. She liked to roam the forest and
explore. She enjoyed the plants, the animals, the rivers and
valleys—everything was of interest and had something to offer.

Apollo first encountered Daphne near a river in the
forest, as she watched a wild sow and a farrow of piglets. She
carried a bow and arrows but had no intention of using them. She
was observing, trying to learn how the animals behaved and
interacted. The little piglets tumbled about, playing with
anything in their path, but always keeping close to their mother,
who gave them time to explore.

After a while, Daphne noticed that she herself was being
watched.

"If you approach slowly and quietly, you can watch them
with me, whoever you are," she said softly.

Apollo was surprised. Daphne looked strong and
independent, but was she really not afraid of a complete
stranger? This was a daring, self-assured women. He liked that.

"They really are curious and playful little critters—
unlike birds at their age, who seem only to worry about being fed
and learning to fly," Daphne said as Apollo got closer.

"They remind me of foxes." Apollo stood next to
Daphne. "I mean, how they play together."

Daphne looked up at Apollo, and with a pleasant smile signaled that he was accepted, while Apollo stared at Daphne with the shyness of a young man. He had never been captivated by a woman. It filled him with happiness.

"They mostly eat plants, but I have seen them eat worms, insects, and even bird eggs," Daphne said.

"I have seen them dig for roots and potatoes. They are quite determined. They even dig for no purpose," Apollo said, immediately regretting it. *Was that too brutish, too negative?* he wondered.

"Families are raised only by the mother. This one still has young males and females. Soon the males will be leaving," Daphne said, unperturbed.

"Sad that the father never stays," Apollo said wanting to be more warm, but also wondering how Daphne would respond.

"Who needs them?" Daphne joked, and pushed playfully on Apollo's shoulder.

Apollo chuckled and smiled at Daphne. He felt their eyes meet for just the right amount of time. Then they turned back to the pigs.

Talking to Daphne excited Apollo. He felt tension, even some anxiety. The anxiety lessened with time, but the tension remained—and it felt good.

Occasionally, he would pause while looking at Daphne, trying to melt his eyes into hers. He had never tried this with anyone before, and it didn't work. Her eyes were quick and strong but never softened for him.

Apollo respected Daphne. Here was a woman that was not afraid. A woman who surely would not be dependent on anyone. A woman to learn from. Full of life. Someone to be with not only because of her beauty, but to experience things with. It felt good just to be around Daphne, as if life was more fulfilled.

Apollo began to visit Daphne every day, and eventually he felt like entering her presence was like stepping into another world. The real world disappeared, and it was only Daphne and he who mattered when they were together. He constantly wanted to do things with Daphne, to be with her. Apollo knew he was in love, and it scared him a little. He was used to being more in control of himself. Still, what did it matter? He had longed for this feeling; now he finally had it and he was going to enjoy it, even if it was a little disconcerting.

One day, Apollo and Daphne were rolling in the grass down a hill dotted with small yellow flowers, giggling. The smell of the grass mixed with the flowers was sweet and intense. It was a beautiful summer day perfected in the afternoon with subsiding heat and a subtle breeze. The setting was so beautiful and their spirits so joyful, that Apollo felt Daphne might be offended if he did not share his feelings. When they stopped rolling, Apollo took a deep breath, looked at Daphne lying next to him, tried again to melt his eyes into hers, and moved closer. Daphne looked at Apollo, reining in her laugh and catching her breath. Apollo leaned in to soften her eyes with a kiss.

Daphne was not prepared for this. Before Apollo touched his lips to hers, she jumped up with a despondent look. She was upset. She liked spending time with Apollo, she liked him a lot, but she could not see herself taking the relationship further. It was as though there was an unseeable barrier, a line that could not be crossed, and if it were crossed, everything would change, giving rise to obligations, to feelings of possession.

Apollo lay in the grass stunned at Daphne's reaction. Why wouldn't she like it if he loved her? However, he realized quickly that she was not ready. He did not want to scare her further, and so he did not get up while Daphne ran away. Apollo's love for Daphne told him that the best thing to do at that moment was to wait.

Apollo did not know that Daphne had acted this way before. She had rejected every suitor before him, because Daphne was afraid of being restrained. Freedom was her most cherished possession. She wanted to experience life fully in her own right, not be held back by another person's love. Apollo's attempted declaration of love was exactly what she did not want. She considered it a request to possess her, not for them to be together. She ignored how much she enjoyed being around Apollo and how much she liked him, and focused instead on how Apollo could constrain her actions. She had no way of knowing that this was all due to the lead arrow Eros had shot her with.

"I don't want your love." Daphne yelled as she ran away, but then she stopped. "Love is about marriage and possessing someone," she said, and looked back at Apollo, awaiting a response.

Apollo got up slowly, trying to look apologetic, not to show his disappointment. He felt that he had been jolted back into reality—like he had just been expelled from the special world he inhabited with Daphne. Why was this coming apart, he wondered.

He walked slowly, timidly toward Daphne.

"Why are you so upset?" Apollo inquired softly. Daphne did not respond. "Are you afraid?"

Apollo explained that he just wanted an accomplice in life, an accomplice like her.

"This is not about having something," he reassured her, still in disbelief.

"You want to possess what you love. That is just how it is," Daphne retorted, then turned and ran away.

Apollo did not run after her. He stood there in shock.

The next day, Apollo decided he could not give up. He went to find Daphne in the forest as he had done every day before. Daphne, now aware of Apollo's feelings, fled every time he tried to approach her. Apollo would chase her, and if he managed to catch up, he would try to persuade her of the sincerity of his love.

Daphne felt every assurance and declaration of love by Apollo to be a hidden restraint. Apollo explained many times that he was the god of many things. He did not need and was not seeking any possessions.

"This is not about me gaining a wife. I simply want to be with you, always," Apollo said to Daphne earnestly.

Daphne considered the privileges of being Apollo's wife, living on Mount Olympus with him. As the wife of Zeus's most important son, surely she would have special powers. But the lead arrow would turn Daphne's focus to the obligations that came with being a princess. She was certain she would not be free to do what she wanted. She might even have to dress the part as opposed to wearing whatever suited her, as she always had. No matter what Apollo said, the lead arrow forced Daphne to interpret it the wrong way. Of course, Daphne did not know that she was cursed with the lead arrow, she just felt its intended impact.

Every time Daphne rebuffed Apollo, the golden arrow framed it as another indication of her free spirit and independence—her zest for life. It made him love her even more. He continued to give chase. Nothing could deter him.

Apollo, too, knew nothing of the arrows. Those struck by arrows were not allowed to know about them. If they did, they might revolt against the gods, or at least against Eros. Feelings so strong were not meant to be caused by a god's whims.

Besides Eros, the only gods who knew about the arrows were Zeus and Hera, who watched the torment Daphne and Apollo suffered but did not intervene. Eros had shot the arrows, and Zeus and Hera respected that.

"Even we gods need to show restraint," Hera would say whenever Zeus felt sorry for Apollo.

Daphne's father, Peneus, was ultimately the one to intervene. He could not watch the ordeal day in and day out. He saw how determined Apollo was and how reluctant Daphne was. When he appealed to Zeus, Zeus told him about the arrows under strict instructions not to tell anyone else, especially Hera. Peneus was devastated, for he understood that his daughter was confined to a misery that would have no end.

The only solution he saw was extreme, but Peneus was sure at the time that it was better for Daphne to have no interactions than to have them consumed with an impossible struggle.

It broke Apollo's heart when Daphne became a laurel tree. The woman who had been fulfilled by roaming the forest, who radiated zest for life, now was confined to passively watching the same spot in the forest for the rest of her life. Apollo felt tremendous guilt.

He also felt a loss he'd never suffered before—the loss of a person he was truly intertwined with. Apollo's first love was rooted in innocence, unimpeded by the realization that it might not last, or that there might be another to follow it. His was the deepest love possible, and when it was torn from him, Apollo was unsure whether he would ever love again.

From that day on he wore a laurel wreath to remind himself of Daphne. Yet eventually, he did move on. He dated Cyrene, a mortal and queen of an African City, but she fell in love with Apollo's brother Ares, and Apollo was devastated again. Then he pursued Marpessa, who fell in love with Idas, ironically fearing that Apollo would eventually not love her anymore. Then he fell in love with Hyacinth, who died tragically, and Cassandra, who simply did not love him. With every relationship—and there were many others—Apollo became more numb, and it became more impossible for him to replicate what he'd had with Daphne. He never took off his laurel wreath. He never stopped longing for her.

When Peneus finally liberated Daphne to allow her to go to Mieza, one of the other river gods witnessed the transformation. It did not take long for the news to spread across Mount Olympus. Everyone knew how Apollo suffered and what an opportunity this created.

It was Eros, who enjoyed spreading mischief, who told Apollo that Daphne was free again. He explained the circumstances, happy to set Apollo on a renewed quest Eros was sure would end in misery.

Apollo had seen Eros' devious ways and did not trust him. However, Apollo did not suspect the arrows. When Eros told him about Daphne's liberation, Apollo embraced him. "Thank you," he exclaimed as he pulled Eros closer, feeling compelled to hug him.

Eros relished the irony.

Apollo was overcome with joy. Daphne's natural curiosity would blossom again. He loved her so much that he focused on the good that was coming to Daphne. He would not renew his pursuit for fear of Peneus turning Daphne back into a tree. Apollo could not let that happen. He had to protect her.

However, in the weeks that followed, all Apollo could think about was Daphne. He wondered what she was doing and fantasized about being with her in Mieza. He tried to resist these fantasies but could not. The effect of the golden arrow was too strong.

Eros would occasionally come to see him and encourage him to pursue Daphne. "What kind of a man are you?" Eros would say. "You won't get another chance. Take the opportunity while you have it."

Apollo thought this a superficial justification. "I can't do it just because I have the chance," he said.

Finally, Eros persuaded Apollo. "Bestow your love. Daphne needs you." *That always gets them*, Eros thought, and he was right.

Apollo proceeded slowly and cautiously in Mieza. He did not know how Daphne would react if she found out he was there. He was sure that, particularly now, her human emotions would be delicate and prone to turn quickly. Relationships sometimes soured on seemingly insignificant things, Apollo knew. He needed to be careful. This was his last opportunity, and he could not risk Daphne's father taking note of his renewed pursuit.

Hoping to avoid their interference, Apollo did not tell any of the gods what role he would assume in Mieza. This was his love and he had to pursue it alone. To allow others to interfere would make it less private and less from within.

Apollo was also afraid that none of the gods were qualified or necessarily had his best interests in mind. He himself was the illegitimate son of one of Zeus' many love affairs—none of which had ended well. At worst, Apollo feared the gods might become jealous of what he might have with Daphne.

3. Arrival in Mieza

Phaenon was the first to arrive in Mieza. His father had arranged
for him to stay in a farmhouse outside of town, together with
Kallos and Perseus. It was humble, but it suited them all. Perseus
did not care; Kallos did not have much money; and Phaenon was
keen to assume a more student-like existence.

Krasi, on the other hand, was staying at the house of a
wealthy merchant friend of his father. "Make a good
impression," Krasi's father had told him when he bade him
farewell. Krasi was not surprised his father was more concerned
about that than whether he would be happy. Krasi would have
preferred to be with the other students, where the action was
likely to be.

Phaenon was greeted at the farmhouse by a hunched-
over older man with narrow shoulders and stringy dark hair.

"We don't get a lot of horses like this here," the man
said, taking hold of the reins.

"I am Phaenon," Phaenon said proudly, after
dismounting his horse with the straight back of an aristocrat, not
the posture of a stable boy. It was unintentional, the type of
posture ingrained through his upbringing.

"I am Argo. I own the farm," Argo said with a stern look.
With someone like Phaenon, he knew he had to establish his
status.

Argo had learned to judge people quickly, and this
judgment had proved vital in many situations. He rarely lost a
bar fight, rapidly assessing whom to stand up to and whom to
escape from. Still, Argo's face showed the scars of the few fights
he had misjudged.

Argo judged Phaenon as someone with a desire to succeed but who didn't know what he really wanted. In Argo's mind, such a mindset was all too common in the privileged, who suffered from a cluelessness that sometimes manifested itself in wicked ways.

"A good horse, not used to the long ride, but it did what it was supposed to," Phaenon said, petting his horse not in a compassionate way, but in a way to emphasize that he was the horse's master.

"You can put him in the front pasture," Argo said, glad to be able to put Phaenon in his place.

Phaenon disliked Argo's stern, empty demeanor. He was used to people attempting to be pleasant to him. Some of the menacing scars on Argo's face also scared him.

"Thank you," was all Phaenon dared say, though he held his back straight still. He then led his horse to the pasture. The horse pranced next to him, aloof to its new surroundings. Phaenon took some pleasure from that. He might have been afraid to show it, but Phaenon felt that Argo and the farm were beneath him, regardless of his desire to live a more relaxed student life for a while. He was glad his horse seemed to agree.

Phaenon walked his horse in the pasture for a while—longer than was necessary. He made sure the horse picked only at the lush green grass and avoided dandelions. He was proud that Argo had noticed his horse's beauty, though he was at least trying to fight that a little. After all, how could he have a vacation from his regular life if he clung to such trappings of success?

Phaenon looked up when he heard a thunderous commotion on the road, where he saw a rising cloud of dust.

Kallos slowed the chariot down just enough to career around the turn into the road leading to the farm. Then he pushed his stallions again to race the last few hundred yards toward the farmhouse, where Argo was still standing.

Argo stood his ground. This was his farm, and he would not get out of anyone's way. It took Kallos's full strength to pull on the horses to a stop in time, but he was pleased by this dramatic end to his journey.

"That was fun." Kallos dismounted, holding the reins and walking toward the front of the horses, who were snorting, shaking, and completely wet.

"You will want to walk that off them," Argo said matter-of-factly. "Our lodging arrangements do not include taking care of your horses. I am Argo."

"Very well," Kallos said, grinning, trying not to let Argo affect his mood. "I am Kallos, son of Plytomy. Pleased to meet you. What a beautiful place you have."

With all the dignity he could muster, Kallos untied the horses from the carriage and led them back to the main road for a long walk. Kallos passed the pasture where Phaenon stood, looking on in admiration. Kallos nodded, and Phaenon reciprocated.

Perseus was nearing the farm as well, on a road overlooking a valley where the river flowed into Mieza. Perseus was sure the gently rolling river would be a place where students could come to let loose. As a tree, Daphne had stood near a river, where she saw many swimmers and even some lovers who would have been horrified to know that they were being watched. Daphne had always envied them. Though watching them had been entertaining, it was not enough.

But that was all in the past. As Perseus, Daphne would pretend to be the son of a newly commissioned general who fought for the empire in distant places to the north. *I can't be from the south or the west where the other students are from, and I can't be from the east where the empire is to expand next. Alexander will ask too many questions*, Perseus thought. *I must be from a distant place in the north.*

"Hello, I am Perseus." Perseus practiced greeting people, trying to get used to this new deep voice. "I am Perseus."

Perseus stopped just in time not to be heard by Kallos, who was walking his horses past on the road. Perseus noted the sweat on the muscular necks of the horses and on Kallos's strong arms and shoulders. Perseus nodded at Kallos in the way one does to strangers one is unlikely to see again, or people one does not want to show too much interest in. Kallos touched his forehead with a salute, gesturing a casual but reassured response. Neither of them knew they would soon be seeing a lot more of each other.

"You must be the last lodger, then," Argo said when Perseus finally arrived. "I am Argo."

"Yes, pleased to meet you. I am Perseus." Perseus gave an inquisitive smile, happy and surprised about being able to carry off the charade so easily. "It is kind of you to take us in. I hope we will not be too much trouble."

Argo blinked several times in surprise; he was not accustomed to such thoughtfulness. "Dinner is after sundown." He showed Perseus where to tie the horse, then led the way to Perseus's room.

Perseus took an immediate liking to Argo, though not because of his pleasantries, which were few. Perseus respected people who had a hard life but kept a good attitude. Argo appeared to have been beaten down more than most, and Perseus interpreted Argo's sternness as a retreat from life. He had given up on seeking whatever pleasant moments life had to offer. Perseus tried to find joy everywhere and therefore took particular note of people who did not.

Kallos, Phaenon, and Perseus finally met around the dinner table that evening.

"Great part of the kingdom here, with all the forests and newly conquered territories," Phaenon said, hoping to get a conversation going. It came off sounding aristocratic, but that was Phaenon's instinct on meeting new people. It was a shield, rooted in the very insecurities that made him so focused on success in the first place.

"Didn't I see you on the road to the farm?" Kallos asked Perseus, ignoring Phaenon's comment.

"Not sure. Long ride," Perseus answered, though it was not true. For some reason, it seemed awkward to admit to having noticed Kallos.

"Rough roads, this far north," Kallos said.

"Hard on that fancy carriage?" Phaenon asked, wanting to show that he knew carriages.

Kallos nodded. "Yes, challenging indeed."

The conversation was awkward, and the three boys were happy when the food arrived and interrupted it.

Argo served fish, olives, and bread, along with an abundance of asparagus, carrots, and cucumbers, which had come from his own fields.

"I have not had vegetables like these in a long time," Perseus said—both to compliment Argo and for self-amusement.

No one, of course, could know how long it had been since Perseus had eaten any food at all.

"No meat," Phaenon said under his breath. Meat was reserved for the wealthy and was a rarity even among the finest houses.

Kallos raised an eyebrow in disgust at the ungrateful comment but said nothing.

After the meal, Phaenon suggested that they should play Petteia—a good way for them to get to know one another.

The game was for two players. Each player placed a set of small pebbles, white or black, on a board with eight rows and eight columns. The players moved pieces horizontally or vertically in an attempt to block the opponent's pieces with two of their own. Each time an opponent's piece was blocked, it was removed. The only drawback of the game was that if both players kept their wits, it often ended in a draw.

"Who plays first?" Phaenon asked as he set up the board.

"I will," Kallos said, "but we need some wine."

He went to find Argo, and came back smiling with a jug and some glasses. "One glass per game, until the wine runs out," he said. "When do we call a draw and move to the next game?"

"You seem confident we can keep our concentration," Phaenon said placing his pieces on the board.

Kallos chuckled. "Or maybe I am good at blocking." In many a horse race, at least, he had blocked opponents from moving past him.

Phaenon nodded. "Let's see."

As they began moving pieces, Kallos started feeling the wine. "I hope we will have some fun with Aristoteles. Not sure I want to listen to all his theories." He told the others he was the son of a mid-level army officer, and had not received the education that might be required.

"What have the rest of us learned before now?" Perseus interjected, hoping to deflect Kallos's self-deprecation. "Math, music, poetry—those won't help us here."

Phaenon turned the conversation to the classmate they were all most eager to meet. "I hope Alexander is relaxed. I won't be able to bear it if everyone tries to impress him."

"Come on, it will be fun," Perseus said. "Let's just enjoy it. You have to admit that whatever happens, it will be different from anything any of us have ever experienced."

"I suppose that is one way to think about it," Phaenon said. "With that attitude you could enjoy anything—even the life of Helen of Troy."

They all laughed.

Helen of Troy's love affair with Menelaus and subsequent love of Paris, was a part of the *Iliad* that most young men did not understand and thus ridiculed. How could Helen of Troy switch between two lovers so easily? Otherwise, of course, the story spoke to them.

"I will check back with you on the fun part in a few days," Kallos said to Perseus.

"You do that." Perseus smiled.

Kallos concentrated on his pieces and quickly won, as Phaenon lost himself in thoughts of what he would say when he encountered Alexander.

Kallos's laugh dominated the room. "Well boys, I guess that means I play Perseus next."

Kallos and Perseus quietly placed their pieces.

A thunderstorm was gathering outside. Perseus could not help listening for the rising wind. It was one of the few things Daphne as a tree had had for entertainment. The bellowing sound of thunder, the glistening strike of lightning, and the drenching rain that usually followed—it was always a spectacle to watch. That it had been one of the few things Daphne could do carried with it some sadness, but from Perseus's body, the memory turned to joy, like a glorified remembrance of childhood.

Perseus also liked watching Kallos. He was engaging and full of action. He exhibited confidence.

Perseus had retained Daphne's the tree's keen observation skills, but that was not sufficient preparation for the concentration required in action. The idea of trapping pieces on the board so they could not move subconsciously also bothered Perseus. It was the worst thing about being a tree—immovability.

Perseus lost the game.

4. Aspirations

Alexander was making his way to Mieza the next day. He rode in a coach with his best friend since childhood, Hephaestion, behind eight horsemen. Alexander, an accomplished horseman, could have ridden alone on Bucephales, a white stallion his father had bought for him when Alexander had managed to tame him at a country fair after most men had failed. But Alexander preferred talking to his friend, so Bucephales' reins were tied loosely to the back of the carriage.

"I shall miss Pella and the Thermaic Gulf," Alexander said.

"It is a great city. I will miss the beautiful temples for Zeus and Hera." Hephaestion had learned to compliment Alexander on his taste, but he also understood that the people Alexander liked most were the ones who challenged him. Alexander liked winners. "Too bad there are no sanctuaries for the kings," Hephaestion teased.

Macedonian culture did not allow for cults around the kings the way other cultures did. While the Macedonian leaders claimed to be descendants of the gods, they never claimed to deserve temples.

Alexander laughed. There was no one else in his life who dared to poke fun at him like that.

"Yes, no temples for rulers. But that doesn't keep us out of Dionysus's sanctuary," Alexander responded with disgust.

Dionysus, the god of wine, was infamously irresistible to women. Macedonians invoked him in rites of passage for men, but also during "bacchic ceremonies," which often ended in what the young Alexander considered unacceptable debauchery. Since women did not participate, men, particularly young athletes and soldiers, were sometimes raped.

Hephaestion knew Alexander was probably thinking about his father, who engaged in such practices. It hurt his mother, Olympias, and was the source of much tumult in Alexander's life.

"They don't really worship the Greek gods this far north," Hephaestion said, trying to change the subject.

Alexander shook his head. "No, they still follow Thracian gods—from what I hear, Dionysius has nothing on them."

"I look forward to learning from Aristoteles," Hephaestion said, trying again to redirect.

But Alexander was still deep in thought. There was nothing he hated more than the tension between his parents.

"Maybe we will start with the *Iliad*." Hephaestion said energetically. It was his and Alexander's favorite—and that of most boys their age.

"That would be great," Alexander said, finally following his friend's lead. "Hopefully, we won't start with that hideous painting they asked me to bring." Alexander smirked, gesturing toward a box on the floor of the carriage.

Alexander's grandfather had commissioned the painting of Pan, the Greek god that was half human and half beast, who tormented hunters and lost travelers. It was exquisite in its realism, but Pan was a grotesque-looking god. The painting was a realistic portrayal of an exceedingly abhorrent thing. Not only was it ugly; it stood for unprincipled mischief and destruction. Alexander could not understand why he'd been asked to bring it.

"If we start with any painting, it should be Helen's abduction by Theseus," Hephaestion said.

"More impressive than Pan, for sure," Alexander agreed.

Alexander and Hephaestion had spent their best moments in the Helen House in Pella, sitting under a large mosaic depicting the abduction. It was their favorite spot, where they went to let loose. Hephaestion understood the pressures Alexander was under—not only the constant fighting between his parents, but also that even though he would one day be king, he had to suffer the difficulties of adolescence like everyone else.

"I am glad we are getting away," Hephaestion declared. "Glad your father insisted."

"Yes, especially from Leonidas."

Both boys groaned. All of their education at the court had been under the tutelage of Leonidas, whose idea of breakfast, as Alexander liked to say, was a long march. The only thing Leonidas had given them, aside from physical torment, was a deep understanding of the methodical military organization and strategies of Epaminodas. Without Hephaestion, Alexander would have found it truly unbearable.

Hephaestion was ambitious at an early age and knew how to foster this friendship with Alexander without the prince noticing his efforts. Hephaestion was protective of their bond. At one point, another son of a general at court had caught Alexander's attention, but before they could form a friendship, Hephaestion made sure Alexander realized that the boy had not won at anything—sports or otherwise. Hephaestion complimented the boy as a "good loser," which was enough to make Alexander drop him. Hephaestion suspected he might have to do the same in Mieza.

Alexander and Hephaestion would stay at an elegant country villa outside of the town. It belonged to the largest landowner of the region, who had been well rewarded for financing many military expeditions for the growing empire. It was small compared to the palace in Pella, but it suited Alexander and Hephaestion—they were eager to be away from prying eyes.

The only other student still on his way to Mieza was Marsyus. Marsyus had the farthest to travel of any of the students: Athens was twice the distance that Pella was from Mieza. In the coach, Marsyus was reading about the myth of the naming of Athens, preparing to meet the great Aristoteles, but the story did not make sense to him, and the constant pounding of the coach was distracting him. *Must they be so careless?* he thought as the coach trundled over another rock and made him lose his line.

He was wedged between two peasants who did not apologize for bumping into him. They had no respect for a boy trying to read, especially since they could not. While Marsyus did not look like an aristocrat, his serious, pointy face that did not require shaving and his piercing eyes made him look like an intellectual. That was enough to make the peasants resentful.

Marsyus did not want to cause an altercation and have to tear himself away from his reading. He tried to find the place where he had left off.

In terms of wealth, Marsyus's family was not far removed from his companions in the coach. Of all the students, Marsyus had the most unlikely background for being invited to be educated in Mieza. Marsyus's father was a sophist, a traveling intellectual who lived off short engagements by students for lectures. It was a poor existence.

Aristoteles and his assistant, Theophrastus, had agreed to have Marsyus as a student only because of his intellect. They were assured that what Marsyus lacked in connections and wealth, he made up for in intelligence. Marsyus knew all the Greek myths and their meanings, as was fitting for a son of a sophist.

What truly set Marsyus apart, however, was his interest in botany. Theophrastus first learned of Marsyus when the boy's father asked to borrow some texts for his son. At the time, Theophrastus refused. His texts were too valuable, and he did not believe that they could be of use to someone as young as Marsyus. To prove him wrong, Marsyus's father came back and handed Theophrastus some papers Marsyus had drawn up, describing a detailed study he had undertaken. He collected mint and gave it to everyone in his neighborhood who suffered from insomnia. He then carefully recorded how it had helped. Theophrastus was impressed by the boy's work and eager to meet Marsyus. He needed an assistant to help him study the medicinal value of plants, and he'd offered the job to Marsyus, as well as a place to stay in his own house.

The myth Marsyus was studying said it was Zeus who wanted to rename the city. Cecrops, the first king of Attica, had greedily named it Cecropia. Zeus conceived of a competition in which Poseidon, the god of the sea, and Athena, the god of wisdom, would present gifts to the city's residents. Poseidon struck a rock with his trident and it produced water, assuring the citizens they would never go without it. Athena struck her spear on the ground and an olive tree grew, assuring the citizens that they would never go without food or firewood. Athena was voted the winner.

Why would the citizens be asked to choose one over the other, when they needed both, Marsyus wondered. Was it yet another one of those choices the gods asked humans to make that had to end in tragedy? It was what Marsyus disliked most about the Greek myths his father had taught him, and maybe why he was drawn to botany. Why were there so few positive myths, myths that could inspire as opposed to frighten?

5. First Lesson

Theophrastus had reserved a grotto outside of Mieza in which to conduct the lectures. King Philip wanted Alexander to be away from the court to learn and become a man. Theophrastus took this one step further and convinced Aristoteles that the boys should be away from everything, to be immersed in nature as they contemplated civilization.

The grotto was an old stone quarry in the middle of a forest next to an open meadow filled with grass but no flowers and a babbling tributary that fed the river that ran into Mieza. It was an idyllic setting. The grotto had been converted into a temple a long time before, and the walls and ceilings were painted with beautiful figures of nymphs. Theophrastus thought the paintings might distract the boys, but the beauty of the surroundings was irresistible.

Four rectangular wooden benches with no backs were placed in two rows behind a podium to create a lecture hall. The new white oak wood of the simple furnishings shone brightly. The straight simple lines contrasted with the usual playful furnishings of a temple and set a rational tone. Tall candles stood on the floor near the benches, far away from the walls—avoiding illuminating the paintings too much.

The musty smell of the cave mixed with the smell of the new wood and that of the candles, resulting in a sophisticated calm scent befitting an intellectual sanctuary. Aristoteles and Theophrastus were happy with what had been created.

Aristoteles, Theophrastus, and Marsyus were making their way to the nymphaeum for the first lecture, with Theophrastus periodically stopping to collect plants.

"There is a great variety of unique specimens here," Theophrastus said to Marsyus as he put another plant into a satchel he was carrying.

"The plants are so different here from the ones around Athens." Marsyus handed a specimen to Theophrastus.

"After the lecture, maybe we should take a walk farther out," Theophrastus said to Aristoteles.

"Maybe," Aristoteles answered absentmindedly.

"Alexander and Hephaestion are only thirteen, and Phaenon is twenty-two," Aristoteles said to Theophrastus. "Such a disparity in age."

"Yes, and none have studied anything useful," Theophrastus said with a sigh. "Except for you, of course," Theophrastus said looking at Marsyus.

Marsyus blushed and bent to collect more plants.

"It may be best to start with stories, stories of the gods, yes? Abstract concepts particularly about virtue won't appeal to them," Theophrastus added.

"Mmm," Aristoteles said in agreement. "I thought I would start with Antigone and Oedipus, start with a story about honor and restraint; that should appeal to them."

Perseus, Kallos, and Phaenon had managed to arrive at the nymphaeum on time, even though they were tired from playing Petteia well into the night and not a little hungover from the wine. Perseus and Kallos had stayed up even after Phaenon had insisted on getting some rest. Perseus could not resist the freedom of being able to engage with someone like Kallos, and Kallos liked the attention.

"Not the place I had imagined to be studying under Aristoteles," Kallos said with a lustful eye on the nymphs.

Perseus and Phaenon tried to ignore him. Perseus felt Kallos was being disrespectful, and Phaenon considered the comment immature.

When Krasi arrived, he joined Kallos in admiring the nymphs. "What a welcome surprise," Krasi joked, staring at the figures.

"Not what I expected, either" Kallos agreed, letting his eyes dance over the figures. One of the nymphs reminded Kallos of a woman he'd seduced after the games in Pieria, but he was not particularly proud of it, so kept the thought to himself.

Alexander arrived with Hephaestion. He had no guards and wore a simple white chiton similar to that of all the other students, except for Krasi, whose white chiton had a shine, most likely from being made of expensive Egyptian cotton. Alexander hoped that the others would soon enough forget his position. He insisted no formalities be directed his way. This suited Aristoteles, who demanded a certain obedience and admiration from all of his students.

Still, when Alexander and Hephaestion walked into the nymphaeum, the other students stared. Alexander lowered his head and smiled sideways at Hephaestion, then whispered how awkward the moment was.

"Doesn't seem like Alexander needs another friend," Phaenon whispered to Perseus. Phaenon was almost relieved, as he still hoped to relax and not to spent too much time in Mieza befriending Alexander.

"I would like to get to know him," Perseus said. "How can you not be interested in knowing the future leader of Macedonia?" Phaenon merely shrugged.

Alexander and Hephaestion sat down on one of the wooden benches next to Kallos, who gave them a confident nod. Kallos, like Perseus, was determined to make as many friends as possible here. He wanted to be popular—or needed to, since he had no family to rely on for his future.

"Nice and cool in here," Kallos said, looking at the water dripping from the ceiling of the cave.

"Perfect for the summer," Hephaestion replied, wary of how nonchalant Kallos was in front of Alexander. It was precisely the type of confidence Alexander would like.

"Seems like the right place," Alexander said, and Kallos nodded and smiled at him.

Kallos rocked back and forth on the bench slightly, but stopped himself from complaining that it was not made for comfort. Kallos could not think of anything else to say.

When Aristoteles finally arrived with Theophrastus and Marsyus, he was a little embarrassed and surprised to find Alexander already there, sitting among the other boys. Aristoteles hated wasting anyone's time. He launched into his lecture right away, even before Theophrastus and Marsyus could find their places.

"Plato, my teacher," he began, "taught that life keeps changing around us, and if we perceive it only with our senses, nothing that is permanent would be knowable. The only permanent world is the conceptual world. You must perceive the world through concepts; that is the only way to make sense of it."

Aristoteles looked around the room with a pleasant smile, well aware that he had to be careful not to be too abstract.

"The concepts we will talk about in my lectures will include morality and justice, but also passion," he continued. "And we will discuss these concepts through the stories of the gods."

He paused briefly and made sure to continue to smile.

"We will spend much time on Plato and his notion of the perfect society—an important subject for the future leaders of Macedonia." He was not above complimenting his students. It was not clear that all of them would hold high ranks in the empire, but Aristoteles wanted them to feel that they all had potential in his eyes.

The students were listening, but also trying to figure him out. What was their teacher like? Did he care about them? Would he chastise anyone who answered a question incorrectly? Or would he be kind and interested in teaching them? He kept his curly light brownish hair as short as his beard, probably so he would not have to bother with it. His evaluating eyes moved quickly over the class. He appeared to be friendly, precise yet open minded, and he seemed to want to build interest in his lectures. Each of them concluded that Aristoteles would indeed be likable, mainly because he looked like he cared.

"We are social animals and need to live together, but we are not all friends. We need rules in our society to allow us to live together when we are not friends. A society that achieves that with the respect of its citizens will persist." Aristoteles looked at Alexander, who made sure not to react, even though the comment made him a little more enthusiastic about the lecture.

"We shall start with Antigone, daughter of Oedipus. Can anyone retell her story?"

All the students knew Antigone's story, but no one wanted to volunteer. Would the great Aristoteles embarrass them? Aristoteles picked Phaenon, since he was the oldest and radiated confidence. Phaenon stood up and told the story.

"Antigone was the daughter of Oedipus, who was the son of King Laius and Queen Jocasta of Thebes. Oedipus's father, King Laius, was told by the oracle in Delphi that his son will kill him, so he abandoned Oedipus with a shepherd to be fed to the wolves. The shepherd did not want to kill Oedipus and instead gave him to King Polybus and Queen Merope of Corinth, who had no son and treated him as their own. When Oedipus himself was later told by the oracle in Delphi that he would kill his father, he believed the oracle meant King Polybus, so he left Corinth for Thebes to avoid doing so. On the road to Thebes, Oedipus's chariot ran into the chariot of King Laius, and the two entered into an altercation in which Oedipus killed King Laius, not knowing that he was his real father. Oedipus arrived in Thebes, where he married the widowed Queen Jocasta, who unbeknownst to him was his real mother. When the shepherd who had taken on Oedipus as a child revealed what had happened, Queen Jocasta killed herself and Oedipus plunged pins into his eyes and ran away with his daughter Antigone."

"Stop there," Aristoteles said.

Aristoteles moved away from the podium and walked behind the benches with what appeared to the students to be an encouraging look. His teaching style and that of the other philosophers in Athens was to ask questions. The theory was that answers were best teased out of students, and that students should learn from each other.

Alexander and Hephaestion were a little discouraged. They thought the lecture had already become too theoretical, and at any rate it was not the *Iliad* beginning they had hoped for. The others were not sure what to think, except for Marsyus, who liked the myth. Perseus, who was generally happy with everything, was glad the lectures had started. Aristoteles noticed Perseus's smile.

"Perseus, can you tell us the meaning of the story Phaenon recounted for us?"

"It is about the defiance of the gods. The more Oedipus tried, the closer he got to fulfilling the oracle's prophecy, ultimately doing just that. Rules set by the gods and revealed in prophecy by the oracle cannot be avoided."

"Good," Aristoteles said with a smile, and walked to the other side of the room. "Though there is the question of why Oedipus should be punished. Was that to emphasize that the gods must be obeyed no matter what? Or was it to emphasize that Oedipus's good intentions were irrelevant, and only deeds matter? Or was it to show that trying to defy the gods ends in self-destruction?"

The students considered these questions, but none replied.

"But let's leave that," Aristoteles said. "Phaenon, please go on."

"Antigone's brothers, Eteocles and Polyneices, took over ruling the kingdom of Thebes from their mothers' brother, Creon, when they were old enough. Oedipus, their father, had said they would kill each other by the sword if they shared the throne. Not wishing for such a fate, Eteocles and Polyneices decided to alternate ruling the kingdom, one brother one year and the other the next. When Eteocles reneged and did not relinquish power as previously agreed, Polyneices laid siege to Thebes to take what was rightfully his. The two brothers fought and killed each other, just as their father had foretold. Creon again became king and decreed that Eteocles should get a formal burial, but Polyneices should not, since he had attacked the city. Antigone objected. Burial rights were sacred, given by the gods, and could not be denied to anyone, she insisted. She defied Creon's decree, buried her brother Polyneices, and then killed herself."

Aristoteles nodded approvingly. "After the injustice done to her father, Antigone said nothing, but after the injustice done to her brother Polyneices, she did. Why?"

Aristoteles called on Marsyus.

"Antigone knows that fate prophesied by the gods cannot be defied, but unjust laws made by men can be," he answered, staring at the ground, a little embarrassed about his enthusiasm.

"That is correct," Aristoteles said. "Antigone teaches us that we need to create a just society. If we don't, its citizens will have the right to ignore its laws, just like Antigone did."

Alexander took note and perked up a little. "A just ruler also has an easier time governing," he said. "My father has a council with a diverse set of opinions and experiences to assure that laws are just."

Aristoteles nodded and asked, "Anyone else?"

"If you are unjust, you can govern with fear," Hephaestion said. "Isn't it easiest to govern with some adoration and some fear?"

Aristoteles thought such a question inappropriate in front of a future ruler, but Hephaestion knew that Aristoteles would like it.

"We are talking about aspirations, not practical compromises," Aristoteles retorted slightly annoyed and not looking at Hephaestion. "So what is this just society? What is justice?" Aristoteles asked. "Polemarchus defined justice as the art that gives good to friends and evil to enemies. Was he right?"

Aristoteles returned to the podium and rested his right elbow on it, leaning toward his students. He had the same encouraging look with which he started the lecture, but there was more urgency to his posture. He wanted the students to think.

Hephaestion spoke first. "Polemarchus can't be right. His justice would mean that whoever is in charge is just—that's not what Antigone taught us."

Aristoteles took note of Hephaestion's quick intellect. "Yes," he said with excitement. "Polemarchus's justice is whatever is in the interest of the stronger. Not entirely satisfying, is it?"

"So how would you define justice, then?" Alexander asked.

Aristoteles turned the question back to the future king. "If you want to be adored by your citizens, what laws would you pass?"

"Laws that let citizens lead a good life, not laws that empower tyrants." Alexander said. "Like the taxes imposed by my father. They have brought protection and infrastructure, allowing everyone to thrive. Others might pass taxes purely to enrich themselves."

"It would make it easier to govern one's citizens, wouldn't it?" Aristoteles responded.

"And to grow an empire," Alexander added.

The lecture continued for a while, with Aristoteles asking questions about what just societies the students knew of, aside from Macedonia, of course. The students discussed the mighty empire to the east, Persia, and the mighty empire to the south, Egypt.

The Achaemenian dynasty in Persia was not a model of good governance, they concluded. Artaxerxes III, the current king, had come to power after one of his brothers was executed for trying to kill his father; then, at the instigation of Artaxerxes, another brother committed suicide and one was murdered. With his throne secured, Artaxerxes had wasted no time killing most of the remaining royal family.

"Not the making of a beloved ruler," Alexander commented.

The Persians had supported the Spartans in the final phases of the Peloponnesian War, which had resulted in Athens losing its empire. Aristoteles would not come to their rescue.

Egypt, on the other hand, had to be admired. Nectanebo II was creating unimaginable wealth and prosperity for his empire. He did this in part by creating stability through military force. He hired mercenaries, stood up strong armies, and successfully repelled continued invasion attempts by the Persians. This allowed Egypt to export their abundant crops of cotton and grain, essentially clothing and feeding not only themselves but most of their neighbors.

"Nectanebo II is loved by his people and hailed 'Nectanebo the Divine Falcon,'" Phaenon commented, wanting to align himself with such an admired ruler.

Still, the students debated about Egypt. They did not want to admire a foreign empire too much. As they would soon find out, even in their tempered admiration, they exaggerated Egypt's strength.

When it was clear they had exhausted the conversation about Egypt, Aristoteles spoke again. "There is, of course, a good example of the ultimate just and good society—the City of Thebes under King Pentheus. We will talk about it and its unfortunate end, in another lecture."

Perseus was satisfied, feeling that the reason for coming to Mieza was playing out. Aristoteles was a strong teacher whose arguments made sense. His way of conducting the lecture and the responses of the students were impartial, analytical, and crisp. Perseus wanted to learn about the world, and lectures like these were perfect. They created a rational framework. *A new world, even if it is derived from stories about the gods*, Perseus thought with a little amusement.

Most of the other students also came around to liking the lecture. Only Kallos and Krasi were not engaged. Kallos fought his interest in the subject, afraid that he was not up to the task given his lack of a prior education. Krasi, quite the opposite, thought the myths to be simplified stories and had no interest on them. "A martyr for the dead," he whispered when they discussed Antigone killing herself after burying her brother. No one who heard him dared to smile.

At the end of class, Aristoteles announced that Alexander was having a get-together that evening for all the students at his house.

"I am assured the wine will be watered down appropriately," Aristoteles joked.

Aristoteles was not particularly happy that the students would have a party so soon after having begun lectures, but he understood that part of being a leader was forging relationships, and Alexander needed to learn to do that. He also respected that students could not be inspired purely by thought. They needed other outlets to grow.

"Looking forward, we will also have some fun with some sports competitions," Aristoteles explained. "In a few days we will start one-on-one matches in a variety of events. The winner of each competition will be crowned with a laurel wreath, just as they do in the games at Pieria."

The student wondered what the competitions would be and which ones they would be chosen for; they had only heard that Alexander was to race Kallos in a chariot race.

The gods on Mount Olympus also wondered about what sporting entertainment might lie ahead. They enjoyed watching games - all but Eros who was by himself. The other gods knew his mischievous ways and tried to avoid him as best as they could. "Let the games begin," Eros said with a snide laugh. "Effort, joy, victory, and at the end, no winners."

"Now we will find out which of them Apollo chose as his disguise," Zeus said smugly, sitting back comfortably on his marble throne.

"How is that?" Hera asked, her suspicions roused.

"When Apollo heard that Daphne had been freed from her laurel tree, he took on human form and vowed to stop wearing a laurel wreath until he is reunited with her." Zeus pointed at the wreath in Apollo's chair. "Whoever wins a sports event and wears a laurel wreath can't be Apollo," Zeus concluded.

Hera looked at her husband with disgust. "You came up with this. A competition with rules that Apollo, the god of sports can't ignore, and that reveal who he chose to be?"

"Perhaps. I might have had the oracle suggest it to Aristoteles." Zeus shrugged.

"You must stop interfering," Hera chided him. "It is not our place, and it never ends well."

6. Leviat

That afternoon, Phaenon made his way to Olynthus, where Leviat lived with her parents. Phaenon generally liked to get things done, but he was not sure what propelled him to see Leviat so early during his stay in Mieza. Why rush? If he rejected her, it would only lead to arguments with his parents. His father would throw up his arms and escape into work. His mother would argue in different ways that no one is perfect, while Phaenon would argue that in a decision as important as a spouse, one should not settle. Then, Phaenon's parents would regroup, quickly find someone else, and the whole thing would start all over again.

Olynthus was the capital of the Chalcidic Federation, which had only been conquered by Macedonia a few years earlier, in one of King Philip's major victories. Leviat's father had the great honor of having been chosen to lead the federation as it was being integrated into Macedonia, his reward for not losing any military campaigns as a general in the Macedonian army.

"Marriage is an opportunity to build our family," Phaenon's father told Phaenon before he left for Mieza. "Families with similar backgrounds, with similar sensitivities," his mother emphasized. Those comments were ringing in Phaenon's head as he made his way to Olynthus. There were few families who would enhance Phaenon's family's status like Leviat's family, and Phaenon chose to interpret his parent's comments to be about that.

Phaenon set aside his simple-student aspirations and dressed for the occasion, hoping to inspire the respect of Leviat's family. He wore a dark red belt with a golden buckle over his white chiton, and new black sandals whose lacings were still pristine.

When he laid eyes on Olynthus, the entire affair suddenly seemed more intriguing. The city was built on two hills in two parts—the southern hill held the archaic city of Bottiaens, while the northern hill was home to the newer city of Chalcidian. What impressed Phaenon most was how Chalcidian was laid out in the modern rectangular Hippodamian system he had thus far only heard about. Large avenues ran north to south and smaller streets east to west. Chalcidian was also fortified with an impressive wall and towers system. This was the Macedonia of the future, and Phaenon was drawn to it.

Phaenon entered Chalcidian with pride. "Where is the house of the governor?" he asked the soldiers at the gate.

When Phaenon finally found Leviat's parents' house, however, he was disappointed. It seemed like no work had been done on the house since it was built, and the old wall that surrounded it was overgrown with vines. A large worn wooden door with rusty hinges led to a courtyard.

Phaenon stood in front of the door and ran the edges of his fingers through the front of his already perfect black hair. He shrugged his shoulders back to make sure his chiton dropped correctly, knocked on the door, and took a step back to wait.

"I am Phaenon," he said when a disoriented servant finally answered the door.

"Are they expecting you?" the servant asked with an accent Phaenon could not place.

"Yes," Phaenon said, self-assured. "Just give them my name." Phaenon did not feel like explaining himself.

He was led through another courtyard to the main house. An archway that led to the garden around which the house was built. Phaenon was asked to wait by a fountain in the center of the garden.

Phaenon watched the water splashing from the top of the fountain into a basin in the form of a seashell. The sound was pleasant, but not enough to relax him.

The garden looked casual with its overgrown pathways, wild uncut trees, and unaligned bushes. It was wet and mostly green, no flower beds or planters to add color. *Not what I would have expected from an army general's home*, Phaenon thought as he played with the water in the fountain. *The garden could use some order.*

Phaenon loved nature arranged in geometric forms. He had insisted on installing formal gardens at his parents' house, of which he would eventually be master. His parents complied because Phaenon had been such a dutiful son.

Just as Phaenon was starting to doubt he had come to the right house, Leviat's father appeared. "Phaenon, I presume," the man said with an intentionally disarming smile.

Phaenon felt obliged to smile back.

"I have known your father for a long time. We were in several battles together. A fine commander. One time, just south of here, I wanted to give the men a break. They had fought for four days straight. He insisted on speaking to all of the battalion leaders individually, and convinced them we could not lose momentum. I think he also convinced them we were close enough to smell the gold that would go to the victors." Leviat's father chuckled.

"He sends his regards." Phaenon was not sure what else to say about the story, which he had not been told before.

"I hear you are studying with Alexander in Mieza. That must be interesting for you."

Before Phaenon could reply, Leviat arrived, led by her mother as though she was a precious object.

"Well, here she is," the father said.

Leviat appeared reluctant and uncomfortable about being presented this way. Her smile seemed forced, but to Phaenon's surprise, it quickly sweetened into an earnest one once Leviat's mother let go of her.

"Do you want to take a walk in the garden?" Leviat asked, before they had even been introduced, or survived the awkward first moments that would have been sure to follow. Perhaps this was the independence Phaenon's parents had told him about.

"If it pleases your parents," Phaenon answered, being overly formal. Leviat appreciated the irony.

Leviat's parents knew that Phaenon was not seeking their permission and smiled. They lingered around the fountain as Phaenon and Leviat walked off, then commented to each other that they thought Leviat and Phaenon had similar senses of humor. They wanted Leviat to find someone compatible and were hopeful that Phaenon could be it.

Leviat and Phaenon were quiet until they were outside the earshot of Leviat's parents. Then Leviat started the conversation. "What is it like in Mieza?" She had a soft yet serious voice, the type people listen to because it demands attention, not because it is high strung or threatening.

"We just got there. We had our first lecture, about the rules of governing a city," Phaenon answered. "A city like this." He stretched out his arms with a confidence that he hoped would make him look aristocratic.

Phaenon was close enough to Leviat to detect the heavenly rose fragrance she was wearing. Leviat must have been eager to meet him, he thought.

"What was the lecture like?" Leviat asked, now allowing herself to look at Phaenon for a little longer with soft, brown, inquisitive eyes.

"We spoke about Antigone," Phaenon said with the same small smile that had been on his face since they left the fountain. "The disobedient one, you know?" Phaenon said. He wondered whether Leviat would object to him criticizing Antigone.

"Will you be studying poetry?" Leviat asked, not taking the bait.

"Not sure. Who do you like?" Phaenon asked, presuming Leviat would not have asked about poetry if she were not interested in it.

"Have you read Hesiod?"

Hesiod was known for subtle, down-to-earth poetry, not the aspirational heroes or love stories most people liked. Phaenon had heard of him but knew none of his work well, and preferred to pretend not to know who he was. He shook his head.

"His *Works and Days* focuses on the everyday," Leviat continued. "You work hard, don't stay idle, and the rest takes care of itself."

Leviat had intentionally mentioned a poet she thought would not impress Phaenon. She wanted him to see that did not matter to her, so that Phaenon would feel comfortable sharing his own thoughts. They were there to get to know each other, not to impress each other.

"Nothing grandiose, eh?" Phaenon said, his smile finally broadening, showing his strong teeth. "What are your goals, then?"

"Family and children," Leviat said matter-of-factly, deepening the unpretentious dialogue.

"I respect that," Phaenon said, nodding, and locked his eyes onto Leviat's to assure her of his sincerity. Phaenon himself had little interest in children, but he was courting.

"Not something I have to hide, then?" Leviat asked.

Phaenon pushed out a brief laugh. "No, no secrets."

Phaenon was intrigued by how unassuming and forthright Leviat was, thought he was not yet certain he respected it.

Their walk was interrupted by a snake crossing the path.

"Watch out," Phaenon said, raising his arm to stop Leviat from walking further.

"It is just a garden snake. We have many of those."

"Don't you want one of the servants to take care of it?" Phaenon asked with a commanding look.

"Oh no, we don't mind them." Leviat continued to walk even before the snake disappeared under one of the bushes.

A snake would have been a disturbance in his parents' garden. A disruption in the order he insisted on. Leviat could not have cared less. There were more important things to worry about.

The rest of the walk they spoke about their upbringing. Leviat's childhood seemed perfect. Both her parents spent a lot of time with her, the only exception being when her father was on military campaigns. They took an interest in her education, including in matters of family holdings, but they also wanted her to have friends and be herself. Leviat had many childhood friends and spoke about them at length.

That was not the case for Phaenon, though he did not admit it. Leviat noted that Phaenon did not speak about any friends at all. His childhood had been focused on grooming him to follow his father into business. His parents doted over him, and Phaenon did not resist. He told Leviat mostly about business matters he'd learned during his upbringing.

Phaenon liked Leviat well enough. But he was mesmerized by Olynthus, so the fact that Leviat was the daughter of the governor was the real pull. This was the type of family he wanted to be part of, and he decided to pursue the courtship.

"So we will see each other again?" Phaenon asked when their walk came to an end. He wanted to be the forthright one this time.

"That would be nice. I have not learned about your secrets yet," Leviat said, though she had begun to make some assumptions about his ambitions. She also meant to imply that she did not have any secrets, even though she did—one in particular that she would not share with Phaenon under any circumstances, for if he knew, he would not court her. Leviat planned to expedite the courtship before he discovered the truth.

7. Alexander's Party

Kallos and Perseus were making their way toward the villa where Alexander and Hephaestion were staying, perched on a ridge west of the city and visible from afar. Torches blazed in front of the house, illuminating the white wall that surrounded the property. Behind the house was a deep valley, and beyond that a mountain blocked out about a quarter of the sky. The illuminated wall beneath the mountain made the whole scene look like a gigantic lantern.

"I have not seen Phaenon since he went to Olynthus," Perseus said as they walked.

"Unfortunate," Kallos said, "being matched up like that when he doesn't need to be."

Kallos was insecure about his status in Macedonian society. This could be fixed with a wealthy or influential wife, he knew, and he did want wealth, a nice house, and the respect that came with that. It was just not Kallos's way to marry for it. He wanted to marry someone he enjoyed spending time with. For status, he would make his own way, and in his mind that started here in Mieza with the other students—especially with Alexander. Who knew where that friendship could lead? He tried not to think about this too much. It made him uneasy.

"I like Phaenon," Perseus said. "He strikes me as the type of person who tries hard to do the right thing."

Kallos did not agree. Phaenon struck Kallos as someone who might do the right thing, only not because he believed in it, but because it got him where he wanted to go. It was an important difference.

"What do you think Alexander will do if I beat him in the chariot race?" Kallos asked. "I think I can win." Kallos flexed his muscles with an enthusiastic smile.

Perseus looked away. That sort of bravado made Perseus uncomfortable.

"Pretty impressive, right?" Kallos went on, throwing his head back with pride. "Me racing the future ruler of Macedonia."

"Did you know that he can trace his bloodline back to Hercules—I mean, the god Hercules?" Perseus said.

"You think that will help him in the race?" Kallos asked, even though he knew that Perseus was trying to move off the subject.

Perseus laughed and then humored Kallos. "I admit it is gutsy to race against Alexander, and I hope you win." Perseus tone was conciliatory but slightly mocking, keeping Kallos at a distance rather than taking the opportunity to further befriend him. "Kallos the Powerful," Perseus joked.

Kallos liked that. He managed to laugh at himself.

When they gave their names at the gate, guards in full dress uniforms waved them through. It made Kallos and Perseus feel special. Another set of guards was stationed at the entry to the house let them pass without further questions.

The house was built as a square around a courtyard garden, much like Leviat's parents' house, only bigger and with the newest materials. A covered walkway surrounded the garden, with Greek columns in the latest style. A servant escorted them under the colonnade to the rear left side of the house, where they could hear the party.

Perseus noticed a marble statue of Zeus at the center of the courtyard that was otherwise unadorned. The statue showed

him with long curly locks and a stern look. It lacked the charm
Perseus knew Zeus had. The garden surrounding the statue did
not have the usual plants and flowers, but a sea of rocks covered
the ground, giving it a striking look. Perseus gave the statue a
small wink and smiled—slightly amused by the thought of a
petrified Zeus watching the life Perseus was about to experience,
wishing he might join the fun.

When they entered the room, Alexander got up from one
of the lounges set up around the perimeter. "Welcome," he said
with a cheerful smile, and raised his glass. "Make yourselves
comfortable. You know everyone."

Phaenon and Krasi had arrived first. Phaenon had been
eager to finally talk to Alexander. Krasi, on the other hand, came
early in the hopes that his assumptions about the party might be
proved wrong.

The northern part of Macedonia was least influenced by
the niceties and mores that Athens was admired for. Wine was
not watered down, and parties were known to end in the type of
debauchery King Philip liked. Krasi himself was hoping to make
his way into this lifestyle. He had been with women early even
for a boy in Macedonia, and his youthful appetite continued to
grow. He was always pushing his limits, seeking something
more.

But Krasi was convinced he would not find it at this
party. Alexander would want to get acquainted, and they had
nothing to celebrate—an excuse often cited for such events. So
far, Krasi was right: the party was off to a tame start, with
everyone gathered around listening to Alexander and
Hephaestion talk about military strategy.

Krasi smiled at Perseus, spreading his uncanny charm. Perseus was someone he wanted to get to know better. It worked, Perseus sat in the lounge next to him.

Kallos sat next to Hephaestion, who sat to Alexander's right—there was no lounge to Alexander's left. Kallos hoped he might at least speak with Hephaestion about athletics, and that that might be a way to strike up a conversation with Alexander. Hephaestion was known in the empire to be an excellent wrestler, one of the few to have beaten Alexander. Kallos thought that as athletes they might have something in common, but Hephaestion ignored him.

Marsyus had not arrived yet. He hated being forced to make conversation, and knew that predicament was unavoidable at the beginning of parties.

Indeed, an awkward silence lingered as they all tried to find their places and size each other up.

"We were just speaking about Epaminodas," Alexander said to keep things going. "My father studied his military strategies when he was a hostage for much of his youth in Thebes. Epaminodas focuses on discipline and organization for winning battles."

"Yes, but I thought we agreed that his tactics are too mathematical," Hephaestion said. "Tactics have to take into account the soldiers at hand and their motivation. I would use different tactics if I had a group of tough, heroic Macedonian soldiers then if I had Greek mercenaries."

"I agree. I also think innovation, not strategy, wins," Phaenon said, hoping to be provocative. "Like your father's use of the six-foot spear formation, the sarissa. That surprises opponents and wins wars."

Alexander nodded appreciatively despite the obvious attempt at flattery. "You must also be an admirer of a cavalry charge to the right of a battle line, then. Slanting the advance with increasing pressure on the front?"

Phaenon nodded.

"It increases the pressure on the other side and never relents until the very end," Hephaestion said, squinting his face to mimic the pressure.

"Then you pursue the defeated relentlessly so they can't retreat and regroup," Alexander added, chuckling at Hephaestion's expression.

"Yes, another great innovation," Phaenon agreed. "Destroying your opponent's passion and not allowing them time to regain it. That finishes them off."

"Passion is key," Alexander proclaimed. "Passion made Achilles the best soldier in the Trojan war. That is why he is a hero."

"But you need both passion and discipline," Hephaestion responded seriously, "don't you think?"

"Yes, I suppose," Alexander said. "Though at times they seem to be at odds. I wonder what Aristoteles would say about that."

"He probably doesn't know much about warfare, and he might get annoyed with us making a 'practical compromise.'" Hephaestion said smirking at Alexander.

"I agree," Kallos chimed in to everyone's surprise. "Passion and discipline matter in most things, just like with good horses."

Neither Alexander nor Hephaestion wanted to talk about horses or the upcoming chariot race. The room fell silent for a moment, and Kallos started to feel embarrassed, even a bit jilted, especially by Hephaestion, who continued to refuse to acknowledge him. Such early animosity would be hard to reverse.

Kallos had learned, mostly on the streets, how to judge people. He figured out quickly that Hephaestion was protecting his friendship with Alexander. This would come to a head at some point, he feared.

Marsyus's arrival was a welcome distraction. Being late, he lowered his head, made sure not to look at anyone as he made his way across the room, and sat down quickly next to Kallos. Marsyus had not gotten acquainted with any of the students, and did not know that Kallos had the least in common with him.

Marsyus overheard the last part of the conversation, and knew what Aristoteles would say, but he said nothing.

"Let's have some music," Alexander commanded.

They had all learned how to play the lyre at a young age, but each had become increasingly reluctant to play it. Playing the lyre was a piece of childhood that could be enjoyed forever, but boys tended to eschew it to prove they were growing up.

"Krasi, you start." Alexander thought Krasi, with his endless smile and confidence, might be the best entertainer among them, and would be the least likely to be offended to be asked to play the instrument. He was right.

Krasi gladly complied, unembarrassed. He played the song he remembered best—a love song. The music started slowly, trying to mimic a subtle feeling, then it became more abrupt, almost like there was something to resolve, until in the third and final piece of the song the melody softened into a delight that made the boys feel a bit awkward. The music quieted the room, took the students to another place, and when it was over required a moment for them to return.

"Thank you," Alexander said after Krasi finished. He did not want the music to linger. Its effect was uncomfortably emotional—too intimate for the group. Then he looked at Hephaestion in a way that let him know that he wanted to leave the party soon. Hephaestion was all too eager to get Alexander away from the others.

The rest of them broke out in conversation.

"How did it go in Olynthus?" Perseus asked Phaenon.

"I did my duty," Phaenon answered. Phaenon did not want to admit he was intrigued by the girl. His visit was a formal matter that should not be discussed with someone he barely knew.

"You did not say much during our discussion," Perseus said.

"They would not have liked what I had to say."

Perseus was intrigued. "Oh, tell me! Sounds devious."

"Not devious, I just think we would do well to study the Egyptians. They have focused on discipline and organization just like Epaminodas. To build pyramids and temples of the sort they do, they not only need good architects but mountains of supplies and armies of people. I think that speaks for organization and discipline."

"I agree," Perseus answered. "But they lead those armies of people by making them understand that the pharaohs are gods —not descendants of gods, but actual gods that need to be worshiped. That is a form of passion, no?"

"Fair point," Phaenon said. "But it is still discipline and organization that makes it work, and they do threaten their slaves on top of making them believe they are gods."

Perseus raised a glass. "Yes, they do. It took us a while to admit the greatness of Egypt in class, didn't it? The strange empire to the south, so different and yet so powerful."

"Our passion for Macedonia got in the way," Phaenon said with the same small grin he'd had for most of his visit with Leviat.

Perseus smirked and took a sip of wine. "Do you believe the rumors that Persia might try to invade them again?"

"They would be foolish," Phaenon responded.

Tiring of Egypt, Phaenon looked around the room. Kallos was speaking to Krasi, but Marsyus was all by himself, looking bored and uncomfortable.

"We should probably liberate him," Phaenon said to Perseus, gesturing at Marsyus. It was an aristocratic and benevolent gesture all in one. Phaenon did not mind showing that he was aware of the characters in the room, while helping the one who needed rescuing.

Perseus laughed and followed Phaenon across the room.

"Did you enjoy the conversation?" Phaenon asked Marsyus, who was surprised to be approached.

"I suppose," Marsyus responded with a shrug. "I did not expect that we would talk about Epaminodas and hear the lyre played all in one evening." Marsyus did not respect Epaminodas, and listening to love songs on the lyre made him reminisce about an early infatuation that had not ended well.

"I hear your father is a sophist. You probably already know a lot about what we will learn here?" Perseus asked.

Marsyus looked at the floor and shrugged again.

"What was it like growing up in Athens," Perseus asked enthusiastically.

"I prefer being in Macedonia," Marsyus responded quietly.

"Really, but there is so much culture there, isn't it the center of things?" Perseus questioned.

"Ever since they lost their empire, it is in decline," Phaenon objected looking at Perseus, and then turned to Marsyus. "Did you know Aristoteles there?"

"No, I never met him."

"So you now get to meet the best of Athens here." Perseus interjected with a smile.

"And the most interesting students," Marsyus retorted shyly.

8. A Walk in Nature

The next day, everyone showed up to the lecture on time. The party the night before had been, as Krasi had predicted, a relatively tame gathering; no one was hungover.

Aristoteles asked Theophrastus to lead a lecture on botany. In the natural sciences, Aristoteles preferred biology and left botany to Theophrastus's expertise.

The group left the nymphaeum for a walk, heading down a path away from town. The early sun shone sideways, creating long shadows and a full spectrum of shades and colors. The leaves on the trees in the sunlight and shade varied from light green, almost white, to dark green. Brightly lit flowers bunched together in places on the grassy forest floor added a rainbow of color.

It was the best time of day—beautiful and full of promises of good things to come, Theophrastus thought as they were walking.

Aristoteles introduced Theophrastus to the class. "Theophrastus is developing a catalog of plant life. You could say he has dedicated his life to it. He has worked on herbivory and poisonous plants, plant pests and use of manure, insect-repellence, seed dispersal, infestations, and much more. Most recently, he has investigated the question of spontaneous reproduction, though we may have different views on that."

No one knew quite what to make of this last comment.

"Thank you," Theophrastus said, his deep voice resonating even outside. "Spontaneous reproduction is the concept that some plants don't seem to come from seed; they are able to reproduce seemingly on their own—without flowers."

Theophrastus smiled at Aristoteles who, realizing how he had confused the students, nodded approvingly.

Marsyus was studying spontaneous reproduction in aloe vera plants, but the rest of the students were more interested in Theophrastus himself than in what he had to say. The teacher put them at ease, and they were not sure why.

He reminded Phaenon of an uncle in his family whom everyone liked but who never succeeded. Krasi recalled people he'd met in his travels who enjoyed the moment while being burdened with a need to prove themselves. Perseus thought the man's constant smile was genuine and came from a happy place that he wanted others to discover.

Theophrastus moved into his lecture. "We are here today to discuss plants. We see plants all around us, and some of you might have noticed that they are different from the plants around where you came from. Why is that? Why are plants not the same everywhere? To solve such problems, we must observe and categorize them. We begin by categorizing plants into trees, shrubs, under-shrubs, and herbs. Then we carefully note their habitats, their form and texture. Lastly, we experiment with how they react to more water, more sun, and different soils. Makes sense?"

Everyone nodded enthusiastically. There was something to be learned here.

Theophrastus stopped his casual stroll and picked up a pod, then walked a few feet to pick a flower. "Here, we see the common bean and jasmine." The students noticed how dirty his hands and fingernails were, but Theophrastus did not seem to care. "Do you know what these are good for?"

The students did not answer. While they felt more at ease with Theophrastus than Aristoteles, they were still afraid of volunteering an answer.

"The bean is good to eat, yes?" Theophrastus said. To illustrate, he pushed some beans out of their pods and ate them with a broad smile. "Delicious!"

The class laughed for the first time. They suspected that class with Theophrastus would be more like an adventure than a lecture.

"We are working hard at figuring out how to better grow plants that feed us," Theophrastus said proudly. "And jasmine, well, it smells nice and has beautiful flowers. But don't eat it. It is poisonous. That is a thing about flowers, they are attractive, but often dangerous."

Theophrastus smelled the flower and passed it around the class. The class handled the flower with care, not because they were afraid of it, but because it felt right to treat anything that was poisonous with respect. Alexander in particular was well aware of rulers being poisoned.

Theophrastus continued while looking at Marsyus. "Poisons do not have to be a negative. Often we can find a medical benefit to poisonous plants. You just have to be careful what to use it for and about the maximum dosage." Marsyus was working on the medicinal value of narcissus, but Theophrastus did not mention it since he was failing.

"Have you catalogued all the plants?" Alexander asked.

"No, but we are trying. Currently, we are studying cucumbers, aloe veras, and cabbage. Did you know they all grow here?" Theophrastus looked around where they were walking, but could not find any. "Well, I suppose you'll have to trust me on that," he said with a chuckle.

"Now, cucumbers are edible like beans, but did you know they like lots of sun and water, sandy soil and react well if you put a little manure in their soil. Aloe vera, on the other hand, though it has thick, juicy leaves, prefers dry, well-drained soil. Cabbage likes sand and clay in its soil, and less water than tomatoes, but more water than aloe veras. Cabbage grows wild in this region, but it has been cultivated into all sorts of different forms in other parts of the world."

"You mean they have different types of cabbage in Persia and Egypt?" Alexander asked.

"Precisely," Theophrastus responded.

"Do you have any?" Alexander asked.

"Sadly, no, but I hope someone will send me some in the future," Theophrastus answered. "Wouldn't that be marvelous?"

"What we have succeeded in, is in making wheat grow more bountifully through use of manure and measures to fight pests," Theophrastus continued proudly.

"That is fascinating," Alexander said earnestly. He knew the benefits bountiful crops could bring to an empire.

Perseus dared to ask a question no one would have dared to ask Aristoteles. "Aristoteles said you are dedicating your life mostly to studying plants. How can you be so focused in your work?"

The class fell silent. They hoped that Theophrastus would not be offended.

Theophrastus responded with his usual smile. "That is a good question. Life has a lot to offer. You will find that there are competing interests. You need to decide what you feel passionate about, what you care about. It may be many things or it may be a few things. In my case, it is a few things—but how wonderful I find them to be! There is a rationality, an order to plant life that I enjoy. Mind you, part of that order is that the gods have allowed us to manipulate plants, to work with them and to change them. If it was solely about categorizing them, I would have a harder time. Find what you are passionate about in life and pursue it. Don't listen to others. If you are passionate about it, it will make you happy."

Theophrastus continued the walk and pointed out different plants as they were walking. The class was mesmerized, especially Alexander. They had not expected this type of lecture.

Why was I never taught about this? Alexander wondered. *It is all around us, ignored until pointed out. To be able to put an order even to that is amazing.*

"We will have another plant lecture soon, and I will show you some of the plants we have grown. In the meantime, I would encourage all of you to pick some plants and bring them to the lecture or to me directly at my home. If I don't have the plant, I will add it to my catalog. If I do, I will explain all we have learned about it to you." Theophrastus looked to Aristoteles.

"Now, in the spirit of the pan-Macedonian games in Pieria," Aristoteles said, "we promised that we would keep your minds and bodies occupied. The first competition among you will be after our next lecture. As you know, it will involve Alexander and Kallos. Kallos came to us from the festival where he won a chariot competition, and despite that, Alexander has agreed to race him."

Phaenon in particular was impressed with Alexander's willingness to oppose Kallos. Yes, he was the future leader of Macedonia, a descendant of Hercules, but the challenge was risky and could prove to be embarrassing. He nodded approvingly at Alexander and Hephaestion, but they did not respond.

Perseus and Marsyus groaned inwardly about the upcoming sporting events. They'd come to Mieza to learn, not to compete.

"I am not looking forward to this," Marsyus said under his breath.

Perseus nodded slightly, and said, laughing, "I like watching, not participating."

"Maybe we are allowed to not be passionate about this," Marsyus said, and laughed as well.

Krasi scoffed and could not make light of it. "Athenian intellectual and athletic concoction," he said in his usual precise way. He was not going to spend time training for any such event. He was going to try to figure a way out of it.

9. Assertive Love

Phaenon sat in his room at the farm. The room was small and dark and had a tiny desk, which Phaenon moved in front of the window to allow for at least some light. He was working on papers for his father's business, which he had spread all over the floor. His office at home had a large table on which he could organize his work properly. Here he had to resort to using every surface.

Phaenon heard a commotion outside the farmhouse but continued to work. He marked some papers at his desk while trying to avoid dripping sweat on them. It was another sticky summer day. Phaenon cursed the work, regretting that he had agreed to do it while in Mieza.

The commotion was a carriage approaching the farmhouse. Phaenon finally looked up from his work, wondering who it might be. When the carriage rolled to a squeaking stop in front of the farmhouse, he got up. Before he got outside, he heard Argo bellow, "There is a visitor for Phaenon." Argo made no extra effort for Phaenon. He had not liked Phaenon from the first day they'd met, and seemed to like him even less now. Phaenon looked through Argo as if he were not there, and never greeted him.

When Phaenon heard Argo, he thought his visitor must be Alexander—the only person he knew in Mieza who might arrive in a carriage. Phaenon wondered what he could want, but was excited about the prospect, which could turn out to be the type of encounter to easily befriend Alexander. He was starting to lose the energy to make Mieza more of a vacation. He walked out of the farmhouse with a straight back and determination in his neck.

To his surprise, it was Leviat, who had come with her maid to visit him. Phaenon slumped and walked slowly toward the carriage, trying to wipe ink off his fingers, annoyed by how sweaty and disheveled he must look. It would have been all right for Alexander—Phaenon would have relished the opportunity to show how hardworking he was—but it was not how he wanted to appear to Leviat.

"Leviat, what a pleasant surprise," Phaenon managed.

"We were in the area and I wanted to see you," Leviat said. "We brought some fruit. I was hoping you would have time for a picnic?"

Leviat wore a peony in her hair, and she smelled of the same rose perfume that Phaenon had admired in the garden in Olynthus. Phaenon considered the red peony symbolizing the blushing of bashfulness ironic, since the uninvited Leviat was anything but bashful. Phaedon did not seek bashfulness—to the contrary, he wanted a woman who could lead with him. The peony was all wrong.

Phaenon did not say anything. He did not know how to react to all this.

Leviat waited, looked at her maid, and finally broke the silence. "If you have other things to do, I understand." Her voice, as before, was precise but soft.

"No, no—I am sorry," Phaedon stammered. "A picnic would be great." Of course, he could not refuse Leviat. She knew that.

Leviat smiled. "I hear the River Arapista, in the hills below Mt. Bromion, is quite beautiful."

Clearly, Leviat had this all planned out. Her determination was a little too much even for Phaenon.

"There is a river within walking distance from here," he said. "It is pleasant and much easier to get to." He wanted to take charge and preferred not to venture too far.

"Fine," she said impatiently.

They walked the short distance to the river in the valley below. The maid stayed a few steps behind them, carrying a blanket and fruit.

Where the river curved small, there was a small sand beach. At the edge of the beach, a patch of wild flowers were struggling to shine. It had not rained in a while, and while they were not wilting, they were not able to push out their flowers. They looked stilted. The most redeeming quality of the spot was how the river subtly caressed the beach.

Phaenon liked watching the parallel ripples in the water as it aligned to navigate the curve.

"A beautiful spot." Leviat said, marveling at the blinding reflection of the water.

She sat upright on the blanket her maid spread out, as though she was holding court. Phaenon sat next to her. He decided not to take off his sandals since Leviat hadn't.

"Do you come here a lot?" Leviat asked.

"No. One of the other students, told me about it," Phaenon lied. He did not want her to think he came there a lot to relax, though he had indeed been there several times.

They spent time talking about a variety of topics, most of them raised by Leviat. Phaenon was happy enough to be with Leviat, but his mind was still preoccupied with work.

"How has school been?" Leviat asked, feigning interest. She was courting as well.

"Fine," Phaenon responded.

He is going to make me do all the work, Leviat thought. "And the other students, how are they?"

"I don't really spend much time with them," Phaenon responded, again short-changing any potential for a dialogue.

"What is wrong?" Leviat asked softly. There must be something in Phaenon's life that they could talk about, she thought.

"Nothing," Phaenon responded, flashing his teeth while forcing the appearance of a smile. "I guess I am preoccupied with things. Besides work for my father, I am also to compete in some sporting events they've organized for us." It was the best Phaenon could come up with. He was sensing Leviat's frustration.

"Are you worried about it?" Leviat asked.

"No," Phaenon responded flatly.

Leviat tore the peony out of her hair and flung it aside. She was done with the niceties and wanted to figure out what was going on. All Phaenon could think was how pleased he was that the offending peony was finally gone. He told Leviat again that he was not worried.

Phaenon stared at the river, contemplating its powerful forces. He thought about tributaries feeding streams, streams feeding rivers until they became majestic instruments. Rivers that fed towns and linked them together. Rivers that may deviate, but always reach their destination.

Leviat stared as well at the glistening powerful water moving downstream with speed. Water near just a minute ago already elsewhere. Moving over rapids or entering lakes. Unstoppable. Restless. Always moving. Until dammed at some point downstream.

Neither spoke of what they were seeing.

Leviat thought about her secret and her plan. She wanted to marry Phaenon, even if he was curt and distracted. She was determined to rescue herself from the increasingly difficult and embarrassing circumstances of her parents, which Phaenon and his parents could find out about any day. Most of Olynthus was already talking about it.

Leviat's father was a respected army officer and politician, but he was not good with money. He had gambled away the substantial sums he'd made from successful military campaigns in a drunken state. It was not only the loss of money but the circumstances in which it had been lost that had put Leviat's family's reputation on the wane.

It was unfair, Leviat thought, that she should pay the price for her father's folly. She'd been brought up with a certain status and had gotten used to it, but it could all come to an end. Phaenon would surely be the last suitor before everyone discovered her circumstances.

Phaenon, meanwhile, was imagining himself as the future Prince of Olynthus. As they walked back to the farm, he tried to carry on a conversation, but it was harder than when they'd met the first time. They spoke about Olynthus, then Phaenon brought up the empire and even Egypt. Anything to keep the conversation going. Leviat was not interested in any of it, but she did her part and humored Phaenon.

They both noticed the superficiality of their dialogue. Nothing pulled them to a deeper level. Both were preoccupied in keeping something going that had little basis.

On her carriage ride back to Olynthus, Leviat resolved to find a way to engage Phaenon. She would not give up. She simply had to be more creative—and more forceful.

10. Choices

Mieza got some much-needed rain a few days later, providing a nice reprieve from the sweltering heat. It transformed the farmhouse from the hot box the boys had learned to endure into a cozy cool shelter. It gave Perseus time to turn to some texts from Aristoteles. Perseus had asked to know more about the "just society," and Aristoteles had offered these materials about the City of Thebes.

Perseus sat at the kitchen table, looking out at the farm in the rain. The fire in the stove did not provide heat, but it made a cozy atmosphere. Just right for reading and contemplation.

Perseus had been missing solitary contemplation in comfortable surroundings. The cadence of the text and the ability to stop and think about it, gave a sense of control one could not have during a lecture.

When the rain subsided a little, Perseus saw Kallos take out the chariot with his horses, casually trotting down the road. Athletes had a swagger that Perseus had always admired and enjoyed watching—the craft, the skill, and the immediacy of sport were admirable.

Perseus turned back to the papers. The City of Thebes had a long history of rulers intertwining the city in conflicts, often by being more focused on themselves than on their citizens. As Aristoteles had said, the best rulers seemed to cater to their citizens. Progress was particularly stilted when rulers fought their own citizens and citizens tried to regain control. But if citizens wanted badly enough to choose better leaders, they did not mind dying for it.

Perseus had just finished the long, twisted tale of infighting about the "Seven against Thebes," who all failed in conquering the city and installing Polynices to the throne, when Kallos returned from his ride.

Perseus watched Kallos as he rode the horses back, calmed them, and unharnessed them. Kallos was firm but gentle with them.

"You did well," Kallos said as he stroked the horses manes. "You know what to do. We are in this together."

It created an atmosphere of mutual respect between him and the horses—respect, Perseus thought, that many of the rulers of Thebes did not have for their citizens.

Perseus decided to set the reading aside and join Kallos in the stables, where he was gently brushing down the horses. The horses had done what Kallos needed; Kallos now did what they needed.

"The horses are not exhausted?" Perseus asked, somewhat surprised.

"Sometimes it is best to ride them for control, not speed," Kallos replied. "Control is important when the race is on a country road as opposed to an oval arena, like the race here."

Perseus stroked the shoulder of one of the horses, gliding slowly down the rippled muscles. "They are strong."

Kallos continued brushing. "Yes, the trick is to harness that strength the right way. I have had horses that were stronger than these that were useless on the race course."

"A lot of things seem that way," Perseus mused, then asked Kallos how he'd come to know so much about horses.

"My father always insisted that I be the best," Kallos said. "I liked horses, and when I started winning competitions, he encouraged me to focus on that."

Perseus listened.

"He never allowed me to get the education I needed," Kallos said glumly.

"Yes, you complained about this when we first met," Perseus said. "It is nonsense. Aristoteles would not have let you come if you didn't belong. You know he believes knowledge already resides within all of us, it just needs to be teased out."

"I am not sure what that means," Kallos responded honestly, which impressed Perseus. Kallos knew what he knew, and was honest about the rest. That showed courage and real strength.

"I don't either," Perseus confessed, "but you handle horses better than kings handle people. We would all do well to study that."

"Thank you," Kallos said, tightening the muscles in his neck and shoulders to produce a thankful nod. His smile was the same as when he'd won the Petteia games on their first evening together. Kallos dominated the barn the way he had dominated the room that evening.

"Where is Phaenon?" Kallos asked.

"I don't know, probably working. He works harder than any of us. He will help build our empire." Perseus responded.

"Remember when we first met him, and he said what a great part of the kingdom this was, as though he were in charge, and then complained about the lack of meat for dinner? I did not like him from that moment. I think he is a conceited aristocrat, and I think he came here for one reason: to befriend Alexander."

"Don't forget Leviat," Perseus added.

Kallos raised an eyebrow, then moved on. "Now, Krasi—there's a strange fellow. That love song at the party?"

Perseus had wondered what Kallos thought of Krasi. Of all the students, those two, thanks to their good looks and charm, had the most experience with women. They were well matched in that department, and Perseus wondered if that created a kind of kinship. They seemed to have bonded over it the first time they stared at the nymphs in the nymphaeum.

"The song was odd," Perseus agreed, and waited to hear more.

"Phaenon told me that Krasi's father became extremely wealthy quickly, and not in the most straightforward way, if you know what I mean."

Perseus nodded.

"Forestry, timber or something," Kallos continued. "Krasi apparently hates his father." He rolled his eyes.

Perseus was surprised to find Kallos so negative about the others. Was it because that was just how he was or because he was insecure, or maybe a little of each?

"And Alexander?" Kallos asked with a slightly mischievous glance. "What do you think of him?"

"I think he will make a great leader," Perseus responded somewhat formally. "He has no pretenses, just wants to learn and seems to be taking it all in."

"He is very close with Hephaestion," Kallos added.

"Yes, I noticed that," Perseus said, looking away.

"Not sure what he sees in him," Kallos said.

"I think Hephaestion is very bright, but dims his light so he will not outshine Alexander," Perseus said. "I like him."

"Well, I think he is weak," Kallos objected. "And you seem to like everyone."

Perseus nodded. It was true. Perseus had taken to Mieza the way Daphne had taken to the forest. Everyone, like everything in the forest, had something to offer. Whether it was incredibly understanding or incredibly naïve, it was rooted in a desire to make the most of things.

Eros, alone as usual, was watching from Mount Olympus. He shifted uncomfortably as he heard this. He liked actions that moved forward swiftly. "Make a decision. You can't like everyone," he said out loud, as though he were speaking to Perseus.

Then he broke out in the maniacal giggle that the other gods on Mt. Olympus hated. "Humans and their precious choices—enough already."

11. Aristoteles's Second Lesson

The students had so enjoyed the lecture with Theophrastus during their nature walk, that they were a bit disappointed to find the next lecture was back with Aristoteles at the nymphaeum. Still, the intellectual rigor demanded in his lessons and the quiet serenity of the candlelit nymphaeum had an appeal all their own.

A sign on an easel was titled "Types of Knowledge," and three circles drawn down the middle were labeled *technical*, *ethical/political*, and *theoretical*. Aristoteles planned his lectures carefully, even if his questions sometimes made them appear random.

"In the last lecture, I told you how Plato thought about knowledge," Aristoteles started when everyone was settled. "Today, I would like to take it one step further. Today we will talk about what the gods know and what they don't know."

"This should be good," Zeus said to Hera. "Let's hear what we don't know."

Aristoteles pointed at the sign and continued, "We divide knowledge into three categories: technical knowledge, involving humans as producers. This involves the day-to-day, the mundane, if you like. Ethical and political knowledge involves how humans organize and interact. This is more difficult to discern. It has to do partly with what we spoke about in the last lecture. Lastly, theoretical knowledge involves truisms, fundamental facts. These are the beautiful principles that are hard to derive, but that are unyielding. Numbers, geographic forms, and virtues are good examples of theoretical knowledge."

Aristoteles moved to the podium and looked at the class. "Isn't it possible that the gods deal only in theoretical knowledge?"

"It would define what the gods care about and what they enforce," Phaenon said, more contemplative than responsive.

"Yes, concepts that reflect the gods, the beautiful," Aristoteles said, holding both his hands out to gesture that this theoretical knowledge was all important.

On Mount Olympus, Zeus smiled at the compliment.

"OK, maybe there are things we don't know or care about, but they are details," Zeus said to Hera.

Hera smiled back at him.

"But the fundamental things, at least he admits that only we fully understand those," Zeus concluded, leaning back in his throne.

He is so easily pleased, Hera thought, but she knew that Zeus was caught up in the moment. *Zeus and the rest of the gods are interested in everything, they are just not supposed to act on it.*

The classification of knowledge pleased Marsyus. "The world of reason," Marsyus said in quiet wonderment, but the class heard it.

"Yes, we can try to figure out theoretical knowledge," Aristoteles said. "We can spend time on it, and in a way get closer to the gods,"

Then he moved away from the podium and started pacing the aisle between the two sets of benches.

"Take that further, and maybe the gods don't concern themselves with how we act within those confines. They actually don't know how humans will act. Don't know and may not care. They may not care as long as we don't break what they set in place—as long as theoretical knowledge or their facts stay intact."

"The gods only care to preserve their confines; the rest is petty," Phaenon said. He liked the order of things that Aristoteles had laid out.

"Not just petty," Marsyus added, "but the more they interfere with us, the more they take away our free will within the confines. That is why bad things are allowed to happen."

Even Krasi liked the construct and joined in. "So the gods don't care?" He felt a sense of liberation in that idea. He did not think of himself as someone who was concerned about such theoretical matters, but he liked what he heard.

"Free actors with confines," Krasi said.

"Well, there you are," Hera said, leaning back in her throne. She raised a glass of wine to Zeus, which was unusual. "You set the order, the rules, some so fundamental, humans can't understand them. They will try and understand some, but not all. Then, how they play within those rules, well that, we leave to them. We are not responsible even when things go wrong."

"Though we may enjoy watching it," Zeus said, and toasted back at Hera, feigning a temporary truce.

Aristoteles moved quickly back to the podium. "Now, we should come back to Antigone and Oedipus. We discussed how Oedipus followed the prophecy of the oracle, even when he tried to fight it. He killed his father, King Laius, and married his mother. Can anyone recall why King Laius received this prophecy?" Aristoteles asked.

"King Laius was raised by Pelops, the King of Pisa. Laius abducted and raped his son," Marsyus said with a shudder.

"That is correct—and the gods punished him by deciding that he would either have no son, or if he had a son, the son would kill him. Oedipus had to kill him to punish him for the rape. So why was Laius punished, but Oedipus, who killed his father and married his mother, was not?"

"Laius was acting in free will, but Oedipus was following a prophecy?" Phaenon asked.

Aristoteles was not happy that Phaenon had responded in the form of a question. He preferred his students to be sure about their answers.

"Yes, it is about free will. Why punish someone who did not act out of free will? What else does the story teach us?" Aristoteles continued, still pacing.

"Well, the only one who was truly punished was King Liaus," Alexander said. "He started the entire saga, though many people ended up suffering because of it. Rulers who don't consider the consequences their actions have on the citizens eventually fail."

"Yes, a great perspective. The story does make that point. Even kings need to mind their actions," Aristoteles said, realizing that he was close to—if not over—the line of what might be acceptable for him to say to a future king.

"But why don't the gods intervene when they see this?" Kallos asked. "They could save the others from having to live with the consequences of King Liaus's actions."

Aristoteles stopped pacing and stood in the middle of the room. "Why should they? Remember, the gods care about theoretical knowledge; the rest should not be important to them."

"Even if it is unjust to Oedipus?" Alexander asked.

"Yes, not in their realm," Aristoteles answered. "And as Marsyus said, if they always intervened when something bad happened, they would take away your free will."

"He is right, mortals should be given their free will to act within our fundamental facts. It is what makes our rules relevant." Hera said to a contemplative Zeus. Zeus said nothing.

"But how does this relate to the just society we spoke about last time?" Alexander asked.

"Ah, an excellent question," Aristoteles said. "It is analogous. Just like the gods have their realm, imagine that all members of society have their realm. Each member with different abilities and tasks. Peasants are peasants and kings are kings. If a society properly rewards everyone's action based on them performing their tasks to the best of their abilities, it is just. My great teacher Plato described this as a meritocracy. The just society is a meritocracy."

"Everyone has their tasks—the gods, the king, down to the peasant?" Phaenon asked.

"Yes, and each is rewarded based on how they execute it."

Perseus was elated. *Yes, the perfect society is a meritocracy. That makes sense*, Perseus thought, then paused. *I just hope Aristoteles is right that this not in Zeus's realm. Zeus might not appreciate him promulgating it otherwise.*

The class felt liberated—they had freedom to act within constraints. There was also no class the next day. It was the day of the chariot race.

Zeus was not upset, but felt constrained by what was being described—even he had a role. Hera, of course, felt vindicated.

Part II

1. The Chariot Race

The night before the chariot race was dark and moonless, unusually quiet for a summer night. Even the insects were silent, as though reverent of what was about to happen. The contests that would reveal Apollo's disguise were about to start.

The only movement at the farm was from the horses in the stable, occasionally snorting and shuffling their manes nervously. Kallos was sure they knew when they were about to be raced. He did not know whether they noticed the tapering of the training before a race, or because he unwittingly treated them differently. The only thing he was sure of was that they knew.

Kallos was awake, lying still in bed and hoping to get some sleep. He was worried about the race. He had the same feeling in his stomach he had before all of his races. It kept him awake, but like other athletes, he hoped it was good for him.

Kallos knew Alexander had been given Bucephalus because he was the only one who could tame him. Of course, riding a horse was different from leading a chariot. But then, why would Alexander's father ask for a race his son could not win? Should he even want to defeat the future king, Kallos wondered, particularly in a race asked for by his father? It would be good to have Alexander as a friend.

It was no use, he could not sleep. As soon as the birds announced the coming sunrise, he got up and went to the stable. To his surprise, he found Phaenon and Perseus there waiting to help him prepare for the race. Kallos appreciated their support.

They harnessed the horses to the chariot, and then led them by their reins to the race course. Kallos explained that he never rode his horses to a race course.

"We walk together, don't we?" Kallos said to the horses. "We are in this together. It creates that essential bond," he said to Phaenon and Perseus. "You lead horses, you don't command them."

When they arrived at the track, Krasi and Marsyus were waiting, and in the distance Alexander was arriving with Hephaestion—both riding in the same carriage drawn by Bucephalus.

"Kallos may just win this," Perseus thought, having watched how Kallos raced his horses the days before at the farm.

Kallos stood tall and led the horses, the three of them as a unit, just like he'd said.

After Kallos checked the harnesses one last time, he stepped majestically up into his chariot. It was hard for Perseus to figure out why, but Kallos continued to look like a winner—relaxed, confident, and in charge. His horses were calm and focused, more calm than Perseus had ever seen them.

Alexander, on the other hand, appeared nervous, and Bucephalus sensed it. Bucephalus twitched and jerked around uncomfortably in his harness. Still, he was an imposing horse, much bigger than Kallos's horses, with bulging muscles all over his body, ready to show their power.

"Bucephalus does not look the way he's supposed to," Phaenon said to Perseus.

Perseus could not look away from Kallos's mastery. It was something to watch and stood in contrast to the usual bluster with which Kallos approached everything else.

And it was in contrast with Alexander, who now was shouting commands at Hephaestion to control Bucephalus. Hephaestion stood in front of Bucephalus, trying to calm him down or at least discourage him from jolting forward.

"You have to be firm," Alexander shouted at Hephaestion. "Don't be afraid of him; he senses that."

Bucephalus stepped forward and backward nervously, almost trampling Hephaestion. He threw his neck every which way and snorted loudly.

"Seems like he just wants to get going," Hephaestion said, giving up on his attempt to control the horse and stepping out of range of his hooves.

Alexander called, "Let's race!" to Aristoteles, who was at the starting line ready to give the signal. "I can't hold him," Alexander yelled.

At that moment, Bucephalus burst forward and started racing down the course even though Aristoteles had not given the signal.

Kallos had experienced early starts before and leaped into action, calmly commanding his horses to follow suit. No complaint, no unnecessary outburst, Kallos just began.

Alexander was a carriage length ahead as the carriages turned to follow a path down into the valley. Kallos did not seem concerned.

Alexander's carriage made loud cracking sounds as it navigated the rough road trying to stay ahead. "He is going too fast," Phaenon said to Perseus. "There are too many rocks in the road."

Kallos let loose the reins, giving his horses some freedom. The horses were finding the right path, but not making up ground from the slow start. They were still behind.

The students ran over a field so they could see Alexander and Kallos as they raced next to the river in the valley. From the top of a hill, they could see that Kallos had managed to get just behind Alexander and was jockeying for a position to take him over. The road was barely wide enough, and every time Kallos came close, they would head into a curve where there was not enough room to pass.

"Kallos appears stronger and in control," Perseus said. Even though his horses were relatively small, Kallos was tall and more muscular than Alexander. At this stage of the race, he also manifested an assertiveness that Alexander lacked. The only thing Alexander appeared to have going for him was his powerful horse.

"Appears stronger?" Krasi said. He was standing next to Perseus and Phaenon, wanting to be part of the conversation, and he was a bit jealous of how intrigued Perseus seemed to be by Kallos.

Perseus said nothing in reply, but started to cheer for Kallos. It caught the rest of the students by surprise.

Hephaestion started to cheer for Alexander.

Phaenon and Krasi joined in, but made it look more like they were cheering for the race than for any particular participant. Phaenon did not want to risk falling out of favor with Alexander, and Krasi did not want to support the person Perseus was so enamored with.

Kallos and Alexander disappeared again, and the students moved back down the hill to a position where they could see the chariots come up the road on the other side.

When Alexander and Kallos reappeared, the two carriages were next to each other. Kallos was on the outside, but they were heading into another curve and Kallos would have to move around Alexander to take him over. Just as they entered the curve, Kallos whipped his horses and pulled slightly ahead of Alexander. It spooked Bucephalus, who was not used to being overtaken, and slowed down for a brief moment. In that moment, Kallos pulled out of the curve and overtook Alexander on the outside.

"So much for their relationship," Krasi said sarcastically.

"You mean Bucephalus and Alexander, or Kallos and Alexander?" Perseus said, smirking.

The carriages disappeared again on the other side of the hill, and the observers moved again, this time to where the race would finish. When Alexander and Kallos reappeared, Kallos was still leading. He was standing tall. Even though he was sweaty and exhausted, he retained his composure. In a serene manner, he harnessed his and his horses' determination to cross the finish line without wavering for even a moment. There were no wasted motions, no unnecessary expressions, no superfluous excitement. Everything was smoothly aimed at speed.

Alexander, however, looked anxious and impassioned, unable to gain control. He tried to corral the energy he and Bucephalus had into speed, but could not. The horse had passion, power, and drama, but it manifested itself in a confused and misguided manner, almost as though Bucephalus was expressing it sideways, all around him, as opposed to directing it forward toward the finish line. Alexander anxiously whipped and screamed, but to no avail.

"Kallos is going to win," Perseus proclaimed cheerfully.

"Only a race," Krasi muttered back.

Kallos safely kept his lead over Alexander but took no chances. He did not slow down at the finish, and neither did Alexander. The crowd ducked and covered their faces as the two carriages crashed by. When Kallos and Alexander came to a screeching stop far beyond the finish line, they were alone in a cloud of dust.

Kallos feared that Alexander might be angry, so he was surprised to look back and see him smiling.

"Congratulations, great job!" Alexander said with admiration, totally out of breath. Alexander thought about saying how proud he was that Macedonia had a horseman like Kallos but did not. He was the future king, and it would have seemed like he was somehow trying to lay claim to the victory. He'd come to Mieza to learn, not to reign, and he respected what Kallos had done.

"I need to get your thoughts on how to lead Bucephalus more naturally," Alexander said enthusiastically.

"Any time," Kallos replied. He wanted to say more but emotion overcame him, and this time he did not fight it the way he had during the race. He had won! He was not sure he belonged in Mieza, but he belonged in Macedonia! No one could deny that. Not everyone might understand that it had taken years of training muscle and mind, but everyone would understand the result.

Kallos shouted a deep, resonating "well done" to his horses. They turned their ears slightly to take it in, knowing they needed to do nothing more.

Alexander, still catching his breath, could only watch uncomfortably as Bucephalus jostled his mane back and forth, confused about what had just happened.

Then, Alexander and Kallos turned their carriages around and rode them slowly back to the cheering crowd.

"A great race," Aristoteles proclaimed when they arrived.

"Kallos took a chance just at the right moment," Perseus proclaimed to Krasi, and then walked over to hold the reigns of Kallos's horses before Krasi could respond. Perseus spoke to the horses calmly, just like Kallos had.

Aristoteles walked between the two carriages, holding a laurel wreath. He signaled for Alexander and Kallos to stand in front of him. It was time to crown the winner.

"Now we find out if Apollo chose to be Kallos," Zeus said joyfully. "Let's see if he takes the laurel wreath."

"I don't think so," Hera replied.

"Why not?" Zeus asked.

"Because I trust that Apollo knows Daphne will be interested in more than good looks. She spent all that time as a tree, watching, observing, unable to move. She will want an exciting life—full of action. Even as a tree she could look at pretty things, now she will want more."

"Give Kallos a little more credit than that," Zeus said. "You saw how he kept a cool head and controlled those horses." He leaned forward on his throne to continue watching.

Kallos took time to shake Alexander's hand. Hephaestion, standing next to Alexander, felt marginalized. All the attention was on Alexander and Kallos. He was not used to that.

"There is a lot of luck involved in races," Kallos said, beaming. "It is not always the best rider who wins." His smile reflected the pure joy of winning, not of winning over someone. This was true sportsmanship.

Kallos smirked at Hephaestion briefly, and with that smirk Hephaestion realized that Kallos had figured out what most had not—Alexander liked winners. It was obvious to Kallos from the moment Alexander congratulated him in the dust at the end of the race that Alexander respected him more now. Kallos had a real chance of befriending Alexander now—which was exactly what Hephaestion was afraid of.

Kallos turned around and looked at Aristoteles. He looked hesitant.

Aristoteles smiled at both competitors. He thought for a minute about how Kallos had showed all of them how to command - decisively but calmly. *Maybe that is why King Phillip requested Kallos to come to Mieza*, he thought, *to teach him how to lead horses or better yet humans.*

He did not want to take too much time with the event and raised the wreath.

Kallos did not move.

"Well, Kallos, are you going to come over here and take your wreath?" Aristoteles asked.

"The race was so close," Kallos said. "Do we really need to crown a winner? We are all students here." Kallos smiled at Alexander.

Alexander widened his shoulders. "Kallos, you are a true sportsman," he said with a broad smile. "Now take your wreath!"

"Yes, take it," Hephaestion muttered. He was ready for this to be over.

"Go on, you won fairly." Alexander gestured toward Aristoteles.

Kallos moved to stand in front of Aristoteles and bowed his head.

"A well-deserved victory, we can all learn from you" Aristoteles said as he put the wreath on Kallos's head. Kallos smiled and all the students applauded.

"Well, you were right," Zeus said to Hera, a little upset that the mystery was still unresolved.

"I suppose so," Hera said with a smile, pleased with herself, and with the fact that the mystery was going to have a more sophisticated solution.

Aristoteles wasted no time announcing the next competition. "Alexander, you now get a chance to redeem yourself. Every contestant gets two chances. The second competition is for you to wrestle Marsyus."

The crowd scoffed a little. The match seemed unfair. Alexander had been brought up as an athletic wrestler, though he'd never beat Hephaestion—who in the last few years had been the only one who dared to wrestle him. Marsyus was a scrawny intellectual who played no sports. The only interesting part of the match might be that there was not much of Marsyus to hold onto.

The match was to occur in a barn where space had been cleared. Aristoteles led the way.

"Alexander would be an obvious choice for Apollo," Zeus said to Hera. "Who would not be attracted to the future king?"

"That is not a bad thought, but if Daphne were attracted to power, she would not have chosen to be Perseus in Mieza," Hera responded.

"What do you mean by that?" Zeus asked.

"Daphne is the daughter of a river god. She could have asked to be a demigod with infinitely more power than any mortal."

"I suppose you are right. Why do you think she did that?" Zeus asked.

"It probably has something to do with the reason *some* gods choose to have affairs with mortals," Hera said.

Zeus ignored the jab.

"There is something intriguing in the frailties and insecurities of mortals that makes life with them interesting. The only question is whether Apollo was smart enough to conclude this on his own."

Though Alexander was disheveled and exhausted from the horse race, he composed himself and managed to appear relaxed as he arrived at the barn.

Marsyus was still at the race course, listening to reassuring words from Perseus.

"Don't worry about it. Try to stay low and take your time. Eventually, he will make a mistake or wear out. He is already tired. That is your only hope. Don't try to overpower him."

Perseus thought Aristoteles might have chosen Marsyus given how tired Alexander was likely to be, but felt that Marsyus could not beat him regardless. Perseus just wanted to help Marsyus get through it.

"I appreciate your support," Marsyus said. "Seems like everyone else is rooting for Alexander on this one."

"Don't worry about that," Perseus said.

When Marsyus entered the barn with Perseus, he focused on the arena, not the crowd. It was a perfect square, cleared and marked with robes strung from stakes in the four corners. Whoever had cleared it had made a special effort to rake the ground with straight parallel lines, which made Marsyus and even Alexander a little resistant to enter. They stood next to the robes that marked the border.

Krasi noted that Marsyus did not even look like he was eager to win. Marsyus cared little about impressing anyone. Even in class when he clearly knew the answers, he would often remain silent. Maybe he felt the same way about the wrestling match. "Obvious Loser," Krasi said to Kallos.

"He is too small." Kallos laughed, straightening his back to seem taller. He also shook his head a little, flaunting his new laurel wreath. Now that he had accepted it, he was proud of it. It set him apart.

When Aristoteles impatiently signaled that the fight was to start soon, Marsyus and Alexander entered the arena and shook hands.

"May the best person win," Alexander said.

Marsyus nodded and walked back to his side of the arena. Then Aristoteles explained that the match would be won by the wrestler who could throw the opponent to the ground two times in a row, or the most number of times in a dozen bouts.

He raised and lowered his arm, the way he had intended to signal the start of the horse race, and Alexander and Marsyus approached each other. Alexander did so almost apologetically, knowing he was much stronger. He grabbed Marsyus by the shoulders and immediately pulled him to his side, rolled him over his shoulder and threw him to the ground. It was over in a second. One forceful precise move, bolstered by the passion Alexander brought to the sport.

"That is one," Kallos said to Krasi, assuming the second was soon to follow.

Marsyus staggered up, realizing he needed to concentrate—not let his mind tell his body that he could not win. He pulled himself together. A surprisingly fierce look came over his face.

"Look who woke up," Krasi said.

Alexander approached Marsyus again and pushed him to the side. However, before he could roll him again, Marsyus pulled Alexander toward himself and almost tripped him. Alexander stumbled a little, then composed himself and tried again—unsuccessfully.

"Not so easy," Krasi said, smiling at Kallos.

The crowd was surprised by how agile Marsyus proved to be. Alexander always lost to Hephaestion because of a lack of agility.

Alexander and Marsyus started their next bout. They got into a clinch, each holding the other tightly. This would test the strength and agility of their legs. They pulled and pushed, but none could get the other off balance. They separated and tried again and again.

Perseus nodded at Marsyus when he looked over for reassurance. It was one of those moments that Marsyus would not forget. Here Perseus was clearly rooting for him in front of all the other students, even though everyone expected him to lose.

Alexander did not look at Hephaestion, or anyone else for that matter. Hephaestion yelled out a cheer for Alexander, but Alexander did not respond.

Alexander summoned his inner forces, his passion and resolve. He had lost once, but he was not going to lose again.

Alexander moved forward to start the next bout with determination. He grabbed Marsyus, rolled him over his shoulder, and threw him to the ground. It was an exact replica of the first bout. It was over in a second, but this time done with such fervor that the crowd gasped when Marsyus hit the floor. There was no way Marsyus could have stopped it. No one could have, probably not even Hephaestion.

The match was over.

When Alexander received his laurel wreath, he shook Marsyus's hand magnanimously. No one thought any less of Marsyus. For a split second they'd thought he had a chance, but in the end, when he lost, it was no surprise.

Alexander stood to the side by himself. Being the future king was lonely. Everything was given to him. Everyone was pleasant to him. Every time he succeeded it was because of his status. This was different. Alexander knew he'd won because of his resolve. He was passionate about wrestling. He never gave up despite always losing to Hephaestion. It was his determination that allowed him to win that day. *It is a great feeling—winning,* Alexander thought. *It gives you a great sense of purpose.*

2. Lesson of Desire

The next lesson came together hastily. Theophrastus was meant to give another nature talk, but it was pouring. The students wore blankets over their chitons to protect them from the rain, but when they arrived at the nymphaeum they were drenched.

The nymphaeum had not been prepared, and none of the candles were lit. The students lit them and then hovered over them to warm their hands and dry off. When Aristoteles and Theophrastus arrived with Marsyus, they joined the huddle.

Alexander said, "At my party, we discussed disciplined soldiers using Epaminodas's strategies versus soldiers driven by passion like Achilles. Which reigns supreme?"

Aristoteles liked it when his students asked questions. The topic was also one he'd expected the boys to raise at some point. Boys like warfare and heroes, they still have exalted notions of both, Aristoteles recalled mentioning to Theophrastus when he prepared for his first lesson.

"By the way you phrased the question, I suppose you realize both are important," Aristoteles responded, walking to the podium and brushing off his chiton. The students took their seats on the benches.

"Of course, but everyone admires Achilles, not Epaminodas," Alexander insisted, looking at Hephaestion for support.

"That is right!" Hephaestion exclaimed.

"Achilles is a hero," Aristoteles said and paused, smiling at Theophrastus. "He is a passionate soldier. So was Antigone a passionate fighter for justice. She did not stand up to the unjust fate of her father, but she stood up to King Creon, who was breaking the rules of the gods. She sacrificed herself, like Achilles. Both heroes acted on their own accord, not listening to what they were told. Both are to be admired."

Perseus was confused. *Theophrastus told us to follow our passions. Now Aristoteles is? I thought he would only respect logic and reason.*

Aristoteles walked into the aisle between the benches. Alexander and Hephaestion were anxious to hear a more complete answer.

Aristoteles paced as he spoke. "However, we have to remember that passion can also lead to bad outcomes. Passion is often at odds with discipline, as you suggest, Alexander, but sometimes it is better for discipline to prevail and sometimes for passion to prevail."

"We should discuss this in the context of the downfall of the City of Thebes, which I promised we would discuss. Phaenon, please tell us about Dionysus, the son of Semele and Zeus."

Phaenon stood up as proudly as he could in a drenched chiton, with his hair disheveled but otherwise not looking much different than when it was dry. "Dionysus was unique among the Olympic gods in that his mother, Semele was a mortal. When Semele became pregnant by Zeus, Hera killed Semele by having her look at Zeus in his godly form, which was not allowed. Zeus then protected Dionysus from Hera by sewing him into his thigh. When Hera discovered this, she had the titans rip Dionysus out and then to shreds. Rhea, Zeus's mother and the goddess of mother earth, brought Dionysus back to life and had him raised by mountain nymphs. When Hera discovered this, she drove Dionysus to madness and caused him to wander the world. As he did, wherever Dionysus went, he introduced wine, and by doing this and by being one of the most sensual gods, Dionysus was always accepted. Eventually, he regained his sanity and was accepted back on Mount Olympus as one of the gods, even by Hera."

"Imagine that," said Zeus on Mount Olympus, teasing Hera. Hera was embarrassed and did not respond.

Eros was listening as well. He was jealous of most of the other gods, but especially of Dionysus and how he'd managed to redeem himself. "Dionysus became boring and unimportant, that's the only reason they like him now," he scoffed.

Aristoteles became impatient. "I want to get to the part about Thebes," he said respectfully.

Marsyus knew why Aristoteles wanted to. The real lesson of Dionysus was in the way he brought down Thebes. But he looked away to avoid being called on.

Phaenon continued. "The one prize that eluded Dionysus was to be accepted in the city of his birth, Thebes. King Pentheus was a law and order king. He brought prosperity and happiness by running the city in a just manner. When he saw Dionysus, he sensed the debauchery he might bring and expelled him. Dionysus would not give up and lured the women of Thebes to meet him outside of the city, and there drove them to such ecstasy and delirium that when King Pentheus appeared to bring them back, they killed him by tearing him into pieces."

"So what does that teach us?" Aristoteles asked, and that time called on Marsyus, knowing the boy would give the correct answer.

Marsyus spoke in his usual shy manner. "Dionysus gave a speech to the women when it was all over. He said that even though people adore order, deep forces reside in them—forces that emanate from their knowledge that they will die. Such forces turned the prosperous and happy masses of Thebes against their benevolent king."

"That is correct, Marsyus. Even if we strive for a just society, we should acknowledge that people are imperfect. There are forces that lead them astray," Aristoteles emphasized.

"Passions?" Alexander asked.

"Precisely. Dionysus teaches us that we have reason, emotion, and appetites. We can reason to devise numbers, geometric forms, virtues etc. But we also have five senses and are bound by time and space. That gives rise to passions that can lead us astray," Aristoteles responded.

He looked around and saw on the faces of students that this lecture was resonating with each of them. They all had passions, some they were proud of and some they were not, but they did not like what they were hearing.

Aristoteles went back to the podium. "Desires, inspired by beauty, for example, can easily cause one to reject reason and overpower judgment. The citizens of Thebes could not sustain their just society because they let their passions run wild."

"But reason should prevail. Surely we can overcome passions," Perseus interjected, not satisfied with how the story of Thebes ended. Most of the class felt the same way. Even Kallos and Krasi wanted a more rational world.

Aristoteles nodded knowingly. "Sometimes, the harder you try, the more you can fail. That is what happened to the citizens of Thebes—the ultimate rational city state."

He knew this was a disillusionment for the class. The rational world they were coming accustomed to in the nymphaeum was coming apart. They'd learned about meritocracy in a just society and thought that humans could be governed with reason, but now they were learning that there was more to consider. Pure emotions, fleeting feelings, could not be avoided. They were an integral part of being human.

The wooden benches creaked as the students shifted uncomfortably. By that time, they had dried off. They looked around at one another, searching for anyone to respond to what Aristoteles was saying.

"Passion cannot be avoided or subverted; it can only be balanced," Aristoteles said.

"But can you argue that Achilles's passion was wrong?" Hephaestion finally asked—suspecting that Aristoteles might find a way, but hoping he would not.

"He was a passionate fighter, and that made him win. We admire that. However, remember, Achilles served King Agamemnon, and had a duty to follow his orders. When King Agamemnon asked Achilles to give his bride to the Trojans to appease Apollo, Achilles's passions bred disloyalty within him. Then, when Apollo, despite that sacrifice, helped Hector kill Patroclus, Achilles's best friend, Achilles's passions boiled over. He fought, but only to serve himself, not King Agamemnon."

Hephaestion and Alexander looked at each other. They admired Achilles and Patroclus so much that in their childhood they had role-played them—Alexander as Achilles and Hephaestion as Patroclus. Now they had to wonder whether Aristoteles was right. Maybe Achilles could still be a hero even if he shifted alliances. Who would not, in those circumstances? Both said nothing and resolved to discuss it later.

"So passion cannot be avoided?" Perseus asked. "You mean to say that we can't live in a rational world?"

"No, you can't avoid passion," Aristoteles responded. "All you can do is temper it."

Aristoteles decided to cut the lecture short in part to have the students focus on this point, but also because he wanted to talk to Theophrastus, who had gotten news that Persia was advancing on Egypt again. If Persia succeeded, it would strengthen them enormously and eventually threaten Macedonia. There might not be an empire left for Alexander to rule. Aristoteles wanted to get all the details.

It had been a miserable day for the students both in terms of the weather and a lecture that had them all questioning what they'd thought they understood. Fortunately, the weekend was ahead and the weather was promising to improve.

3. Ambiguous Plant

The first thing Alexander noticed in Theophrastus's house was a table holding three plants near the rear of the main room. Since Theophrastus's lecture, Alexander had become interested in learning more about plants, so on the weekend, he went to see what Theophrastus was researching at his home.

The main room was the most disorganized space Alexander had ever seen. There were plants on shelves, windowsills, and the floor, and sacks of earth and jugs of water randomly dispersed throughout. The whole place had a moldy, earthy smell and would have been impossible to clean. Spiders had spun webs between pots and the floor. Mice were sure to be hiding somewhere.

The only clean area was the top of the table in the rear of the room. Even there, candle wax had spilled onto the table and a variety of books. Some of the books were open, with pages weighed down with stones. It was on this table that three identical plants were displayed—prominently and cleanly. No earth had spilled from their pots onto the table.

The plants had hairy, green double leaves with a reddish moisture inside, suspended on stubby, brilliantly green stems. Alexander saw that some of the leaves were almost completely shut, and on close inspection that flies were trapped inside.

It shocked him and he took a step back.

The plants did not have pretty flowers and surely were not worth eating. They were small ugly plants with a pungent odor that seemed to trap flies.

Alexander moved closer to study the plants again—as close as he dared.

"Drosera—Venus fly trap," Marsyus said, approaching Alexander. He had not answered the door when Alexander had knocked, but stayed in his room hoping that whoever had come to visit would go away.

But when no one answered, Alexander had let himself in. He had come all this way, and he was not going to pass up the opportunity to see what Theophrastus was studying.

"Fascinating creature, if that is what it is," Alexander said, getting a little closer to the plant.

"They eat flies. I found them in a meadow in the forest," Marsyus said with more self-assurance than was usual for him.

"So they eat flies the way frogs do?" Alexander asked.

"More slowly, but yes," Marsyus responded. "You know how Aristoteles and Theophrastus categorize everything into plants or animals? This one Theophrastus says defies categorization."

"What does Aristoteles think of that?" Alexander asked, speculating that he had stumbled on something important.

"Theophrastus has a running argument with Aristoteles about animals acting with purpose. Here you have a plant arguably acting with purpose or at least eating an animal. He has not shown it to Aristoteles yet, and I am not sure he should."

"Why not?" Alexander asked.

"I think it would introduce unwanted ambiguities." Marsyus smirked.

"I suppose it would," Alexander said, smirking back. "Interesting. I never knew plants like this existed."

They watched, hoping to see one of the plants trap a fly.

Plants that defy characterization—repulsive but functional, Alexander thought. He liked the functionality in things, whether in military weapons, in crops, or in this ugly plant.

"So you live here with Theophrastus?" Alexander asked, looking around the room.

"Yes. In exchange I work on the medicinal value of plants," Marsyus responded.

"That should be interesting," Alexander said, surprised by Marsyus and taking a liking to him. Marsyus knew the myths better than anyone in class, but he had also found a subject beyond that that captivated him. Here was a humble student working away in the shadows, excelling without being noticed or making a point of it.

"Any medicinal value in these plants? Alexander asked. He wanted to keep the conversation going, which was challenging. Marsyus did not look at him and made no effort to engage with Alexander the way most people would. Of course, this only further intrigued Alexander.

"I doubt it," Marsyus responded and shrugged to imply that he did not care. There were plenty of other plants. "Anyway, Theophrastus is more concerned with why plants grow and which ones make for good crops. His interest in these is limited to their strange behavior."

"Well, if there is any use for them, I am sure Theophrastus and you will find it," Alexander said.

As he waited again to see if they could witness the plants capturing a fly, he confided in Marsyus. "I thought it was a bit unfair for them to match you with me in the wrestling match. My tutor, Leonidas, had me wrestling Hephaestion since I can remember. You held your own, though."

Marsyus waved off the compliment. "Don't worry, it was not your doing, and there really isn't any sport I am good at."

"The competitions will not all be sports. There will be a poetry competition. Hephaestion requested that," Alexander said. "He is already working hard at a poem regarding warfare. He won't share it with me yet. Also, Krasi apparently asked to play Petteia."

"*Krasi* asked to play a board game?" Marsyus was astonished.

"I was surprised, too, but Krasi convinced Aristoteles that a game that tests the endurance of the mind should be allowed. Leave it to Krasi, to charm Aristoteles."

Alexander saw Krasi as a charmer—someone who is pleasant to be around, maybe because he had no ambitions except to enjoy the day. Judging people was a trait his father insisted Alexander practice. It was important for a ruler.

Alexander and Marsyus went back to watching the plant, but no flies were trapped.

"Do you mind if I take one of the plants? Would Theophrastus mind?" Alexander finally asked.

"Please take it, but what are you going to do with it?" Marsyus asked with a rare smile.

"Never mind," Alexander said mischievously. "Thanks, Marsyus." He took a plant and left.

4. The Swim

Krasi, Kallos, and Perseus planned to spend their day off swimming at the river. It was a particularly sticky day, one of those days best fought with a swim in cool water.

They followed a road lined with bright wildflowers yearning to be noticed. They ended up at the same bend in the river where Phaenon had taken Leviat. It looked the same, except that the flowers, nourished by the recent rain, exhibited their beauty with a broad spectrum of colors, though they were too far to smell.

Kallos was excited. He took off his clothes and pranced into the river right away. He had no shame, quite the contrary. "The water is nice," he yelled back before jumping in completely. Perseus tried not to look.

Perseus wondered what was appropriate in this situation. As Daphne, Perseus would not have been allowed, but it seemed natural for Perseus to be there.

"What are you waiting for?" Krasi asked as he too took off his clothes. His intriguing face, constant smile and wild curly hair, Perseus thought, made up for an otherwise surprisingly average body.

To avoid the impression of staring, Perseus undressed quickly, ran into the water, and jumped in before Krasi.

"What are *you* waiting for?" Perseus yelled at Krasi to get back at him.

Krasi smiled and proudly walked into the water, submerging himself slowly. "I told you this is nice." He swam to the middle of the river and treaded water, waiting for the others to follow.

Perseus was not far from Krasi, lost in thought. Perseus had come to Mieza wanting to be educated by Aristoteles and meet the future elite of Macedonia, never expecting to be in uncomfortably enjoyable situations like this one.

Perseus watched the water flow down the river from within. Smooth round puddles moving subtly around turns and inlets, caressing gently ,never stopping. Glimmering unstoppable forms moving without force whether watched or not, building ripples only when touched and then releasing back into the flow. Subtle strong currents playing below the surface. The river flowed in a private, insatiable way. It was beautiful and worth exploring.

"Hello! Perseus!" Krasi yelled. "Class is over." Krasi pushed Perseus under.

Perseus, submerged, grabbed Krasi by his ankle and pulled him under until they both reached the bottom of the river. Then Perseus pushed off the bottom toward Kallos.

"That should teach him," Perseus thought, though the attention from Krasi was not unwelcome.

"So you are doing a foot race," Kallos asked when Perseus surfaced nearby.

"Yes, better than Petteia," Perseus said loudly after Krasi surfaced.

"Game of the mind," Krasi responded and chuckled.

"Are you glad it is over? That you won your competition?" Perseus asked Kallos.

"Yes, it felt good, and Alexander seemed to respect it," Kallos said.

"Yes, he seemed almost happy that you won," Perseus said. "I hear he had a big fight with Hephaestion—maybe you could become his friend."

"Not interested," Kallos said. Kallos was proud, too proud to lose to Alexander and too proud to admit it would be good to be friends with the future king. In a way it helped him deal with the feeling he was still harboring that he did not belong in Mieza.

"Isn't that why most of us are here, to befriend Alexander?" Perseus asked. Perseus felt like teasing Kallos.

"Not Krasi," Kallos said splashing Krasi with water. "He is not here to learn or get close to Alexander. He is here to have fun."

"Correct," Krasi responded proudly. "But fun includes making friends," he said in a more serious way.

"Too bad Phaenon was not able to join us," Perseus said.

Kallos rolled his eyes. As he had told Perseus before, he did not like the overly ambitious Phaenon.

"Absentee friend," Krasi scoffed.

When Perseus had tried to persuade Phaenon to come with them to the river, Phaenon had complained about how much time he was going to have to spend pursuing Leviat, on top of all the work he had to do. "The right woman from the right family," he called her and told Perseus how impressive Olynthus was. Perseus actually became a little jealous and wondered what it would be like to have someone to court. It would add a new dimension.

"Boring fellow," Krasi said, mainly because he did not like Phaenon getting attention when he was not even there.

"I don't think he is boring," Perseus objected. "He just has a lot of commitments."

Phaenon had stayed at the farmhouse to tend to some papers he just received from his father. At that moment, he was lying on his bed looking at those papers. The bed, the floor, and his small desk were completely covered with them.

"Why do I have to bother with this?" he thought. He worked some more, but his frustration grew. It was so beautiful outside and hot in his room. He regretted not going swimming— it was a missed opportunity to befriend the other students. Finally, he threw the papers in his hands to the floor, lay back on the bed, and tried to think of the fun he could have.

After a few moments, to his complete astonishment, Leviat opened the door to his room, letting in sunshine and a jolt of fresh air. She was wearing several tiny red roses in her hair and a burlap sack. That was all. The thought of her body brushing up against such a coarse material drove Phaenon crazy. He did not know what to say, but even if he had he could not speak. Leviat did not talk either. She walked slowly toward him with a serious face, staring at him with her soft brown eyes. No smile. Her hair was matted and her lips were bare. She looked like a farm girl, not like the sophisticated young woman he'd met before, yet he liked it. Then she started to dance in front of him. Why? She danced in her burlap sack—not a dress, just a sack pulled over her thin, delicate body. Was she in trouble? Had her parents disowned her?

Phaenon woke up in sweat. He was upset to find it was only a dream, but also happy to have had it. Somehow it made him feel manly. "I like these dreams," Phaenon thought, and lay there reveling in the lingering warmth of the dream. It made up for having missed the day at the river.

When Kallos and Perseus finally came back to the farmhouse, it was dark and they went to their rooms to sleep. Unlike Phaenon, Perseus had a hard time falling asleep, and reflected on coming to Mieza. Lately, it felt like something was missing. It was not enough anymore to entertain philosophical thoughts.

The desire to prove oneself that Perseus first noticed when becoming mortal had grown to include an ever-increasing desire for acceptance. Perseus was making friends—Kallos was one, Phaenon started to share private thoughts, and even Krasi seemed to be making an effort. But it was not enough. Perseus wanted that feeling that seemed to define humans and that even the gods coveted—that feeling of sharing an intimate relationship with another.

What was this desire to be vulnerable? Why was it accompanied by fear? How could one feeling be both scary and desirable? Was it a form of escapism or liberation? Should it be balanced or kept in check? Would it continue to grow? Could it ever be fulfilled?

5. The Wooden Box

When the students arrived at the nymphaeum for the next lecture, they were surprised to see a small wooden box on the podium. Krasi was the only one who dared to walk up to it and examined it, but even he did not dare open it.

"Leave it alone. It is not yours," Phaenon said. "I am sure Aristoteles will explain."

At that moment Aristoteles walked in. "You wonder what is inside the box," he said, while Krasi was still near the podium.

Krasi took his seat while Aristoteles strode to the podium.

"Our mind has an insatiable desire to know. You know that the term *philosopher* means lover of knowledge, but I believe it is not only Theophrastus and I who are philosophers— we all are. We all have that insatiable desire to know. Prometheus stole fire from the gods and gave it to us in the form of knowledge, technology, and civilization; and now, even though we should be grateful, we can't get enough."

Looking over the box in front of him, Aristoteles called on Krasi. "Krasi, please tell us the story of the mythical box. I am sure you know what I am referring to."

Krasi knew the story well. He stood up but kept a crooked and relaxed posture as he told the story—disrespecting it.

"Pandora was the first woman on Earth. The gods created her. Hephaestus created her from clay, shaping her perfectly. Aphrodite gave her femininity, and Hera taught her crafts. She was created right after Prometheus had stolen fire from Mount Olympus for the people on Earth. Zeus wanted to punish the people for that.

"You bet I did," Zeus said, looking over to where they had raised the rim around the flame so he would not have to be reminded.

"And you did a good job," Hera said. "And I did my part." She was glad she had something to compliment Zeus on, and to remind him of her part. Zeus so often dismissed her value.

Krasi continued. "Zeus ordered Hermes to teach Pandora to be deceitful, stubborn, and curious. Then Pandora was given a box and was told it was full of gifts, but she was not to open it. Hermes took Pandora to Epimetheus, Prometheus's brother, to be his wife. Prometheus had advised Epimetheus not to accept anything from the gods, but when he saw Pandora's beauty, he could not refuse. Pandora tried to tame her curiosity, but at the end she could not control herself. She opened the box, and all the curses the gods had hidden inside started coming out—first, seven flatterers that plague us: honor, pleasures, riches, gaming, taste, fashion, and false knowledge; then seven evils: envy, remorse, avarice, poverty, scorn, ignorance, and inconsistency."

Aristoteles was surprised that Krasi knew the myth so well that he could even recount the list of flatterers and evils. *Has he thought about these hardships, has he experienced them maybe by watching his father? But why is he so casual about the myth?*

Krasi had thought about the hardships. When he first heard the myth, he was young and he had indeed witnessed many of them in his father. Subsequently, he learned that most could be avoided by living one day at a time. That is what he now tried to do.

"Go on," Aristoteles said when Krasi stopped.

Krasi especially disliked the next part of the myth, but straightened out a little and then recited it. "Pandora was not mischievous and tried to close the box as fast as possible, but only locked one thing inside—hope. That was actually Zeus's will. He wanted people to suffer without hope in order for them to understand that they should not have accepted the fire Prometheus stole for them."

Krasi sat down. Hope was something he was trying to give up, but he found it hard. Unlike most, he'd prefer if it were locked away in the box. It would be easier that way.

Aristoteles asked, "So what does this tell us?"

"That curiosity is a bad thing," Krasi joked.

Aristoteles smirked, but waited.

Krasi went on, "No, I think it tells us that sometimes it is best to leave things alone. That you should not defy the gods."

Aristoteles was surprised by Krasi's incomplete answer. There was so much to talk about, particularly regarding hope, but he suspected Krasi knew that and did not want to talk about it. He did not want to torment the boy.

"Let's switch to Torin and Keelycael—a short, to-the-point story most of you are probably not familiar with," Aristoteles said. "Torin was a lord of the underworld, responsible for death and disease. Whatever he touched died. Torin's curse was that he also craved nothing more than physical contact. Needless to say, as a result he spread death and disease with a vengeance. Keelycael was a powerful deity who wanted to make Torin atone for the deaths he caused and to end his destruction.

She spent a lot of time with Torin trying to persuade him. At the end, Keelycael fell in love with Torin, much to her surprise."

Phaenon was first to speak. "That is so sad. Keelycael wants Torin, Torin wants Keelycael, but if they touch Keelycael dies? They have no hope of ever being together. No hope of any relationship, any future."

Aristoteles nodded. "Yes. The tragedy for Torin and Keelycael is that they can't have the hope that is locked in Pandora's box, in this case hope of ever being together."

The story irritated Perseus. Even though Daphne had not been able to love Apollo, she'd cared for him. The story brought back the moment when Daphne had been turned into a laurel tree. Daphne and Perseus would be haunted forever by Apollo's shock and utter devastation as he realized that the deep love he'd never felt before, was disappearing, never to return. Apollo was so innocent, so young and open minded, and Daphne had watched some of that die right in front of her.

I will never forget that, Perseus thought. The fact that Torin and Keelycael both wanted a relationship was at least some consolation. Apollo could not accept it, but Daphne had never wanted that relationship.

"Perseus may end up like Keelycael," Zeus murmured. He, of course, knew what Perseus could not: that the golden and lead arrows had created the complete hopelessness between Daphne and Apollo. Zeus hated these dilemmas when they involved love affairs—they hit too close to home.

"Tempted to intervene again?" Hera asked, realizing how upset Zeus was. "Don't even think about it."

Despite that, Zeus resolved to speak to Eros. Eros did what he was told on occasion and then proved useful, but he was a conniving character. Zeus did not forgive him for what he had done to Apollo but suspected Eros might know of something useful for Apollo's predicament. It would be just like Eros to know something and hide it.

"You need to let this run its course." Hera emphasized. "Don't be soft like Prometheus. Don't meddle. It is ungodly."

"Prometheus," Zeus said and got his back up. "The little thief."

"Prometheus is not so little in their eyes. Mortals use the fire he stole well, though they just can't get enough," Hera said. "Prometheus felt sorry for them, and see where it led. Now they want more. Mortals always want more. Leave Perseus alone."

Zeus knew Hera was right, but he couldn't look away from Perseus' sad eyes. He would have felt sorry for Apollo as well, if he weren't still trying to figure out which student he was.

Before the lesson ended, Krasi could not resist asking Aristoteles, "So . . . what is inside the box?"

Aristoteles smiled and opened it. "Hope, of course. You may find it to be a mixed blessing, just like Prometheus's fire. For hope unfulfilled leads to misery of its own."

6. A Different Gathering

Perseus, Marsyus, and Krasi met up on the way to another party Alexander had organized. It lifted their spirits to again see the house illuminated with torches against the backdrop of the mountain, but there were fewer torches. This time the scene looked as though the lantern that the house resembled had been dimmed. There were fewer guards posted at the entrance, and they wore war as opposed to dress uniforms. The scene was less grandiose, as though Alexander did not want to impress or did not want to call attention to the party.

"Do we have to go to these parties?" Marsyus complained as they were approaching the house.

"Marsyus, the model student," Krasi joked. "The rest of us take the lessons to get away from home and party while our parents proudly tell everyone that we are in school with Alexander."

Perseus was surprised by how charming Krasi was even in sarcasm. It was hard not to be drawn to his bright energetic face. The constant smile sometimes bulged his cheeks and tightened his forehead so much that Perseus thought it looked manic, but in a good way.

"I am interested in what Aristoteles has to say," Perseus said, trying to tease Krasi.

"Perseus, student and passionate swimmer." Krasi laughed. "Anyway, tonight we can be whatever we want to be. This is a real party—unlike the last one. They hired musicians."

When they got closer to Alexander's villa, they heard music coming from the garden behind the villa, tantalizingly slow and intimate.

"Do you know this music?" Perseus asked Krasi.

Krasi shook his head. "Provocative, isn't it?" They fell quiet and listened.

The few guards at the entrance to the villa seemed unusually relaxed. They were also listening to the music and smiled as guests approached—not standing at attention the way they had before. A servant welcomed them and pointed them to the garden.

Lounges had been placed there, but everyone was standing, talking, laughing. It was noisy.

"Welcome," Alexander said to Perseus, Krasi, and Marysus, turning away from Hephaestion and Phaenon.

"Send my thanks to your father for the wine," Alexander said to Krasi. "Tell him we have not watered it down."

Perseus and Marsyus looked at each other, surprised to know that Krasi had helped organize the party.

Phaenon was already drunk. The undiluted wine gave him an excuse to let loose even more. They were not used to such potent wine. He raised his glass as he looked at Krasi speaking to Alexander.

Hephaestion stared at Kallos, proudly wearing his laurel wreath. Since the chariot race, Hephaestion had done all he could to keep Kallos from being around Alexander. Kallos was boisterous and drunk, projecting himself more than he should given he was at Alexander's party and exasperating Hephaestion's resentment.

"Having fun is a family matter," Krasi finally said to Alexander. In truth, Krasi was annoyed that his father had intruded on his time in Mieza through the gift.

"Well, I hope you have fun tonight," Alexander said to him and rejoined Hephaestion and Phaenon.

"Your father donated the wine?" Perseus asked Krasi.

"Anything to ingratiate himself," Krasi said. "As you said, everyone wants to be Alexander's friend."

Krasi walked over to where a servant was dispensing wine from one of three large stone jugs, more than could be consumed in one evening. He waved for Perseus to follow. The servant handed each of them a glass cup of wine.

"Drink up," Krasi said.

Without the water, the wine felt like nectar. What it lacked in refreshment, it made up for in taste, Perseus thought. "Is the wine from the North?"

"Just like me," Krasi responded.

When Kallos came over, he asked Krasi if he'd hired the musicians. He had not. The two flute players were the only women at the party, and they were extremely beautiful. It was not customary to have women at these parties, but musicians were an exception.

"They are the closest I have seen to living nymphs," Kallos said enthusiastically.

"Not interested," Krasi said as he watched Perseus walk off to speak to Phaenon.

Kallos was surprised. He thought that Krasi would be the first in line.

Perseus found Phaenon. "So, are you enjoying yourself?"

"Yes, maybe a little too much. I am drunk," Phaenon responded with fleeting eyes, surveying the party, glad to be sitting for a little bit.

"Good," Perseus said the way an elder might.

"What do you mean, good?" Phaenon asked.

"I think you work too hard. You should have some fun," Perseus responded amiably.

"I am tired of being perfect," Phaenon responded, raising his glass and taking another sip of wine. "I hate it." Phaenon had tried hard to let loose in Mieza, but he was failing. He continued to work for his parents, he dutifully saw Leviat, and he had skipped the day swimming at the river. Why was life so hard for him?

"You have a great future, taking over from your father," Perseus said.

It was precisely the comment Phaenon did not want to hear, at least not at that time. "It comes with a price. Always, 'Phaenon do this, Phaenon do that.'"

"But you haven't married," Perseus said earnestly.

"No, I want the woman I marry to be perfect. They at least owe me that," Phaenon said.

Perseus was taken aback. Phaenon had said he was going to pursue Leviat. Had he abandoned that? Was she or her family not perfect enough? Perseus said nothing. This was not the place. They fell silent and listened to the haunting music.

Finally, Krasi joined them. "Good discussion or mutual admiration?" Krasi laughed. "You can't have both."

"Nothing important," Perseus answered a little too quickly.

"Always serious, both of you," Krasi said.

Phaenon decided that, for once, he was going to let the night guide him as opposed to him guiding it. He joined Kallos standing in front of the musicians, trading smiles with them while swaying with the music.

"Not sure what got into him," Krasi said as he watched Phaenon with Kallos.

"I hope I did not upset him," Perseus said. "He deserves to have a good time."

"He will be all right. No matter what, he will be all right," Krasi said.

Perseus agreed. "He will probably have the greatest future of us all, except for Alexander, of course. He just needs to be careful not to have the focus on his career become a form of escape."

"His parents adore him," Krasi said. "Mine just want me to go away. Not that I care."

"That can't be true," Perseus said gently. It was unlike Krasi to show such vulnerability.

"Never mind, this is getting too serious." Krasi changed his tone abruptly. "Where's the fun? A nature walk with wine?" Krasi raised his glass. Before Perseus could respond, Krasi swiped one of the wine jugs from the serving table.

Perseus laughed. "You really are pretty funny."

"Come on, follow me," Krasi said.

The night was beautiful, and the party did feel a little stifling. Krasi could not be refused.

"I know a beautiful field just beyond the villa's grounds," Krasi said.

As they left, they watched Phaenon and Kallos smiling and cheering the musicians. By this time, the musicians appeared to be performing more for them than for the other guests.

The only one not having a good time was Marsyus, who was standing by himself, just waiting for an inconspicuous moment to leave. Perseus noticed this but said nothing.

"Where are Alexander and Hephaestion?" Perseus asked.

"They retreated already. Alexander had to hold Hephasestion back from telling Kallos to simmer down. He hates him," Krasi said. "You know Alexander and Hephaestion prefer to be alone together anyway."

Krasi and Perseus walked out of the villa grounds and down a county road until they came to a large boulder in front of a field.

"Nice," Krasi said, and they sat down with their backs against the boulder.

The field was beautiful, lush with a little moisture on it and full of beautiful wildflowers. Both took a deep breath. They stared at the flowers for a while.

"So why did you really come here?" Krasi finally asked.

"You mean you don't believe I came here to learn from Aristoteles?" Perseus answered, laughing.

"Not really."

"What about befriending Alexander?" Perseus said, still laughing at Krasi. "Is that a good reason?"

"No, you are not the type," Krasi said.

Perseus felt Krasi deserved an answer, but the answer had become more vague as time passed.

"To experience life," Perseus said, and immediately regretted it. "Sorry, that sounds strange."

It was true, of course. There was so much more Perseus had grown to want than just logic and lectures, but what exactly was it? "Life" covered it, however strange that sounded. It was the desire to have a life with all its many facets that was growing in Perseus.

"Not at all. That is what I want to do." Krasi looked straight at Perseus with his big brown eyes and fell silent.

"You have experienced a lot . . . romantically," Perseus said.

"It hasn't been perfect," Krasi responded.

Perseus had never been with anyone. This was starting to weigh heavily.

Krasi saw Perseus's sad face. "You are great. Just relax; the rest will take care of itself." Krasi looked at Perseus just a little too long.

Perseus's mind was racing. What was this all about? Why had Krasi suggested they leave the party together?

Just then, they heard Kallos and Phaenon coming down the path next to the field with the two musicians. They were loud and drunk.

Krasi and Perseus quietly pushed themselves around to the other side of the boulder so they would face away from the path.

"Do you dance as well as you play?" Kallos said to one of the musicians, who was wearing Kallos's laurel wreath slightly askew on her head. He put his arm around her shoulder, and she smiled without answering.

"Of course they do," Phaenon said in his usual commanding way but with a clearly drunken voice. "They are artists."

He was walking behind with the other musician, who gave him a look that showed that she read the situation correctly.

She was aware of everyone's drunken state and that the night was only to provide a reprieve for the students, nothing more.

Perseus watched Kallos, wishing to be more like him at that moment. Kallos was so confident. Perseus was sure it had to do with his looks. Looks were something Perseus had not considered important when assuming the form of a student at Mieza. Now, though, Perseus regretted it. Looks did matter.

"What a beautiful night," one of the musicians said with an empty smile.

"It is," Phaenon replied, stumbling again.

Kallos just smiled and drew the other musician closer.

After that, Krasi and Perseus could only hear chatter and an occasional laugh as the group disappeared into the night.

"Well, that was unexpected," Perseus said.

"Phaenon is still uncommitted," Krasi said.

Perseus nodded and noticed that Krasi was staring again.

"Even Phaenon can live in the moment if he allows himself," Krasi said.

"Do you really live in the moment as much as you say?" Perseus asked, making sure to look away.

"I do, probably too much," Krasi said and looked away as well. "Though more people should. Life is easier that way."

"That is what everyone likes about you," Perseus said. "You are so honest, and you don't make any excuses."

"Well, thank you," Krasi said with one of his charming smiles.

"But how do you strike a balance? I mean, between enjoying yourself too much and worrying about your future?" Perseus asked.

"Relax. If you have to think about it, it is not in the moment."

"To be honest, it scares me a little," Perseus said.

Krasi looked away. He looked at the flowers in the field. They were beautiful and, in the daylight, would have exhibited the full range of colors. At night, their colors were muted, almost like they wanted to hide and blend into the grass until the morning—like animals afraid of the night. *One does not pick flowers at night,* Krasi thought. *Not when they are not parading their colors.*

"Well, then, you should probably ease into it," Krasi finally said.

Perseus did not know what Krasi meant by that but relaxed and stared into the distance. They both decided to focus on just enjoying the beautiful night.

From Mount Olympus, Hera was watching alone. Zeus did not care for Krasi. His impulsiveness reminded him of Dionysus. But Hera liked him. Krasi had a personal code she'd witnessed time and time again. He never got into relationships that he thought could hurt the other party. The girl he had slept with on his way to Mieza was a good example. Krasi, when they first met, had ensured there were no false expectations. Krasi managed expectations appropriately in all of his relationships, and wouldn't push anyone into something they would regret.

Part of being focused on living life in the present for Krasi meant not creating a conundrum in the future. *Isn't it funny how Krasi is better than Zeus that way?* Hera thought, vowing never to repeat it aloud.

7. Aristoteles's Setback

Aristoteles's lectures grew increasingly ambiguous. The logical foundation the students had coveted only a few lectures ago was coming apart. It was a shock to them when news arrived about the potential defeat of their model empire, Egypt. Nectanebo the Divine Flacon was losing to the Persian leader, Artaxerxes III, the barbaric leader who had murdered his family.

Artaxerxes had failed eight years prior. Egypt had a strong navy on the Nile and various canals linking fortified cities. But Artaxerxes had managed to capture the Western Egyptian city of Pelusium, and Nectanebo had fled to the southern city of Memphis, leaving his other fortified cities to fend for themselves, which they almost certainly could not do.

Aristoteles went to Pella to learn more. He was hopeful that with his depth of knowledge in history, politics, and the sciences, he could be helpful. When Aristoteles arrived, the court in Pella was certain that the thirty-first dynasty of Egypt was at an end. Things were tense and dysfunctional.

"The grain and gold of Egypt will strengthen Persia. It will take time, but eventually we will have to reckon with them," Alexander's mother, Olympias, told Alexander when he arrived. "That is what makes this most upsetting."

Aristoteles wanted to see King Philip, but the king found no time for him. King Philip was already being briefed on the situation and believed Aristoteles could have nothing to add.

Aristoteles was left to spend time with Olympias. Naturally, the conversation turned to Alexander.

"I was glad when my husband decided that Alexander should be educated away from the court," Olympias said.

This came as a surprise to Aristoteles, who'd thought it was King Philip who wanted Alexander away from his mother.

"He should not witness the debauched tendencies of my husband, particularly at festivals," she told him. "The king can't control himself. But it may be too late already. Perhaps he has seen too much."

Aristoteles did not believe virtue and restraint could be instilled through lectures. "Good leaders are formed by instilling good habits, not by lecturing to them," he'd told Theophrastus when he outlined his first lecture. He did not know how he would help in this regard, but he promised Olympias he would try. "I will find a way to address this," he told her and meant it.

When Aristoteles made his way back to Mieza he was burdened with listening to Leonidas, Alexander's tutor. King Philip had asked Leonidas to go to Mieza with Aristoteles to brief Alexander about the events in Egypt. For the entire journey, Aristoteles was stuck listening to Leonidas's military theories. Aristoteles found the conversation insufferable.

The man's mind has so much discipline in it that it can't maneuver, Aristoteles thought.

To make things worse, Aristoteles injured his back during the ride. He was in pain and exhausted when he finally climbed the stairs to his house in Mieza.

Aristoteles had a small house, but it suited him. It needed to accommodate only him, and he did not need a house to impress. The front door entered straight into the main room. A large table and two smaller tables formed a straight line at the end of the room, arranged by topics Aristoteles was working on. The table on the left contained papers regarding moral questions, mainly notes from lectures from Plato and ancient texts he was lucky enough to get copies of. The table in the middle contained papers on mathematics, astronomy, and physics—topics of theoretical knowledge that bring one closest to the gods. He thought it was fitting that that table was in the middle. The table on the right was dedicated to biology and botany. Besides papers, it also contained some plant specimens.

It was on this third table that Aristoteles saw a red and green plant someone had put there in his absence, right in the center of the table. Whoever put it there had wanted him to notice it.

Aristoteles had been hoping to read texts he'd brought from Pella, but the plant immediately distracted him. Aristoteles was disturbed by it. The plant was like a strange ugly weed with a proud upright position. Aristoteles stared at it for a while and then noticed a fly caught between two of the hairy leaves.

"Strange," Aristoteles thought, tightening the lines on his forehead. "Did the fly fall into it?"

He put his finger on one of the leaves and nothing happened. But the second time he touched it, the leaf closed. A fly caught this way would not be able to escape. Did the plant attract flies to capture them this way, he wondered.

Aristoteles opened the shutters in the hope that some flies would enter the room. He pulled up a chair and sat in front of the plant for a while. A few flies came in, but they were attracted to the food in the house. Aristoteles covered the food, then sat down in front of the plant again.

As he was waiting in front of the repulsive plant, Aristoteles thought about his unsuccessful trip to Pella. *I suppose sometimes priorities dictate that academics be ignored,* Aristoteles thought with a sigh. But that was wrong. He was sure he would have had something to add to the discussion if King Philip had only invited him.

He also thought it strange that King Philip had not seemed eager to find out how Alexander was doing. Aristoteles's father died when he was a child, and he was raised by a guardian. It was hard for him to accept a father who would not take time for his son. Alexander did not have the charmed life people believed he had, as far as Aristoteles was concerned.

After an hour of careful study, a fly approached the plant and got caught.

"Unbelievable," Aristoteles said quietly. Not much amazed him, but this was highly unusual. The plant had trapped the fly. And judging from the decimated body of the other fly, it would digest it.

"It catches and eats flies!" Aristoteles said this time loudly into the room, slightly pushing back on his chair and releasing the tension in his forehead. He barely noticed the pain in his back when he moved.

However, his excitement quickly changed to disgust. *What a vile plant*, he thought. Plants grew unconsciously, passively; animals ate plants or other animals, and humans had reason and acted with purpose to eat animals or plants. That was the order of things. This plant refused to conform. It ate an animal—attracted, confined, and consumed a fly.

This brings into question the distinction between plants and animals, Aristoteles thought. Aristoteles was distraught. Not only had he felt disrespected in Pella, but now it seemed like some of his and Theophrastus' thinking on plants was being challenged—by one of the plants itself! Aristoteles knew that this could ultimately mean progress, but he couldn't help resenting that it negated some of the work they had done.

Aristoteles had an urge to go see Theophrastus but decided against it. He wanted to take time to contemplate what this meant. He was not sure what he should say to Theophrastus yet.

Another fly was caught by the plant. Aristoteles closed the shutters. It was too much.

Only gods live in perfection, Aristoteles thought. *Their world is black and white and we are meant to discern it and emulate them. We are to figure out what they put in place and make the best of it.*

Then Aristoteles corrected himself aloud. "No, but if the gods live in perfection, there is a lot that does not make sense about them. Why did Zeus seduce Leda as a swan or Europa as a bull? Why did Hera take baths to restore her virginity? The gods do strange things that make little sense. Maybe this plant has to be put in that category."

Aristoteles stopped himself again. "No, no, no. I can't accept that some things don't make sense. Our classifications either work or they don't. If we want theoretical knowledge, we can't have imperfections."

Ambiguity was anathema to Aristoteles. His work depended on eliminating it. Theophrastus had often told him he would be a happier man if he accepted it more.

8. Leviat

Olynthus and the surrounding areas were covered in a haze as Phaenon made his way toward Leviat's parents' house on an unusually dark and cold day. Phaenon dressed in a white robe decorated with a fancy belt and wished he had worn a shirt under it. He shivered and tried to shrug it off as he approached the city gates. He wanted to be seen as a strong, self-assured potential prince of the town. A glorious summer day would have been more appropriate for his arrival, he felt.

As he passed through the city gates, Phaenon greeted the guards as though he was known and walked assertively to the house. His brisk walk helped him keep the cold at bay.

Phaenon continued to believe that Leviat was right for him. She was from the right family, was intelligent and assertive, and could help him run things. He even thought he could make mistakes around her. She had made it clear that he did not need to prove himself.

Unfortunately, he had made a mistake he could not forget. The night at the party. Phaenon thought about it a lot. He had come to Mieza wanting it to be a vacation of sorts, but that longing had evolved into something else. He was overcome with an indescribable feeling of wanting to be a more complete, self-assured, and calm person. It was a feeling that made no sense but was there, always there. He wanted to be more casual and easy like Kallos seemed to him. That is why he'd spent the night with the musician, but it had not helped. He still had this feeling, and he felt anything but calm and complete. He felt unsettled.

Even if no one ever found out about the night with the musician, being caught was not really the issue—wasn't he free to do what he wanted? Yet, he could not shed the thought that he had done something wrong. Instead of liberation, he felt imprisoned in a new self he was not happy with.

"I have not seen you in a while," Leviat said when they were alone in the courtyard of her parents' house.

"I was preoccupied, busy. I am sorry." In truth, Phaenon had been avoiding her, needing time to digest his mistake and taking time to divert himself with other matters.

"I am glad you are here now," Leviat said with her usual soft smile.

They spoke about what was happening in their lives. Phaenon tried to bring energy into the conversation. He longed to feel the tension, the back and forth of when they'd first met. Their last time together, the time that Leviat had come to visit him in Mieza, had been awkward — the awkwardness existed even before his mistake, but it was now harder to move past.

"What was it like when you moved to Olynthus and your father became governor?" Phaenon asked, and then worried whether Leviat might recognize his own ambition in the question.

Leviat ignored the question. "It is fine if you are busy, but I would like to see you more." Leviat did not have much time.

"I said I am sorry," Phaenon said gruffly.

Leviat was taken aback, but she consoled herself, knowing that Phaenon was by far the lesser evil to the financial ruin of her family.

"I said it was fine," Leviat snapped. She hadn't meant to sound harsh, but she was upset.

Both of them understood that something was missing in their relationship since their last encounter. Neither had ever been in love, so they didn't know what was missing—the mutual subtle desire to be with the other person, the trust to share, the willingness to be intimate. Oblivious to such feelings, they were both focused instead on what status their relationship would bring. So much so that even if they had known what was missing, they would have ignored it. In a strange way, that gave their relationship a chance.

Neither of them said anything for a while, as each listed to themselves the reasons the match was a good one.

"I came here to study under Aristoteles, and that is going well," Phaenon finally said.

"Yes, that's nice. But you spent so much time in class and tending to your family's business. I want to spend more time with you." Leviat knew this was no way to court Phaenon, but it just came out.

Phaenon did not react. He thought about his parents, who had similar arguments and spent less and less time together. Over time, their love for each other had lessened to mutual respect. When they'd said goodbye to him before he came to Mieza, they both gave him advice but ignored each other. They stood in different parts of the room, and he felt he was the only thing linking them together. To his knowledge, neither of his parents had done anything wrong like he had, but they ended up there nevertheless. Then he descended into thinking about his mistake again.

"I don't know what to say," Phaenon finally admitted.

After a moment, Leviat softened her tone. "Let's spend more time together."

She could not stand the way he looked away from her. His failure to engage with her was getting to her. She started to wonder whether her secret plan was worth it if it involved Phaenon.

At the same time, Phaenon continued to be consumed with the guilt of his evening with the musician. He was not proud of what he had done. He hated it. He tried to defend himself by thinking about the fact that he was free, free to do what he wanted, still unmarried, still uncommitted. It did not help.

Then he thought about how Leviat was accusing him of not spending enough time. *How dare she demand that at this point? Why is she trying to make me feel bad? Why does she criticize me? Is it her right?* The more fault he found with Leviat, the less guilty he felt. *Can't she respect what I need to do and who I am? Do I need to justify myself to her? Can't she leave me alone? She just does not understand.*

Phaenon left soon thereafter. He was not sure he wanted to see Leviat again, and Leviat was not sure she wanted to see him. The only hope they had was to accept each other's shortcomings, whether by reason or by love. And it seemed there was little chance of it happening by love.

9. A Disconcerting Lesson

The class was surprised to see Aristoteles sitting in a chair next to the podium when they arrived for the next lesson. He had arrived early, not sure how long it would take him to walk to the nymphaeum. His back was still bothering him, and he looked miserable—slumped over and weak.

The students walked in quietly and settled quickly into their places. Aristoteles appreciated this show of respect. It helped him turn his attention away from how upset he still was about wasting the one thing he felt he never had enough of—time. The trip to Pella had been such a failure.

He put a fatherly smile on his face, tilted his head slightly, held out his hands and shrugged to gesture that nothing could be done about his condition. When he began the lesson, he spoke softly, almost as if he was having a regular conversation with the students.

"As you know, I was just in Pella. The entire palace, from the king down, is worried." He did not admit that he had not seen the king. "It looks like the Persians won a decisive battle near Pelusium. We are told that Nectanebo did not have good generals and is retreating."

The class was attentive—more so than usual, further disappointing Aristoteles. He had been teaching about eternal things, and now that he was speaking about an event that would likely be forgotten in history, they were keen to learn more. Nevertheless, he continued. "Persia is asserting its might."

Alexander did not want to hear it. "They are a bunch of bandits! Thieves led by a murderer."

"They may be weakened by having to subdue too many regions," Aristoteles said.

"No. This will strengthen them," Alexander insisted. As Leonidas had drummed into him, Egypt was a dominant trading empire. Their importance and wealth would be useful to whoever conquered them.

Aristoteles knew that as well, of course. "They are far away," Aristoteles retorted.

"Just look across the Aegean—their empire starts right there," Alexander said defiantly, scoffing at Aristoteles. It was disrespectful.

Aristoteles did not want to argue about warfare, especially with Alexander in his current state. He recognized the passion of youth and the predicament Alexander was in. He also knew that sometimes the best teaching involved letting his pupils resolve things for themselves.

Aristoteles changed the subject, giving Alexander a slight, almost apologetic nod. "Well. Let's continue our lessons. I want to discuss Psyche." And Aristoteles took the unusual step of reciting the story himself.

"As we all know, Psyche was beautiful beyond words, even when the gods compared her to Aphrodite. It made Aphrodite so jealous that she asked Eros to make Psyche fall in love with the most monstrous-looking person on earth. When Eros was himself struck by Psyche's beauty, he accidentally wounded himself with the golden arrow and fell in love with her. Prophecy had foretold that Psyche would be taken by a creature on her wedding day, and so it happened that on a hilltop on her wedding day the wind carried her off to a palace. Psyche went inside the palace and saw treasures beyond her belief. When she finally went to bed in the palace, exhausted from her travels, a man entered her bed and they fell in love. Her new husband told her that the only obligation Psyche had was to never see his face. When Psyche returned to see her sisters and told them about all the treasures and how she loved her husband, the jealous sisters convinced her that she needed to see her husband's face. Eventually, Psyche lit a candle in the middle of the night and saw that her husband was one of the most handsome men she had ever seen. A drop of wax from the candle awoke him, and he realized that Psyche had seen his face. The one thing she was not allowed to do, she had done. Psyche was banished to the underworld, away from her true love. So, what is this story to tell us?"

Aristoteles looked at Phaenon, hoping for him to answer, but Phaenon was distracted thinking about how he, like Psyche, had spilled wax on his potential relationship with Leviat.

"Psyche and her sisters were too beguiled by her husband's wealth?" Kallos offered, though he suspected he had not grasped the full story.

"Maybe, but we are told they truly loved each other," Aristoteles responded.

"Did they?" Perseus asked. "If they had truly been in love, there would not have been a need for Psyche to see her husband."

"Isn't that asking a lot of Psyche?" Aristoteles asked.

"Probably," Perseus responded. "I suppose there is a physical element. It may not be possible to love someone who you can't see."

Perseus was, of course, thinking back to the time when Apollo could not see Daphne as a tree.

"Yes, but we can learn more from Psyche," Aristoteles responded.

"Trust," Hephaestion exclaimed. "It is about trust."

"Yes," Aristoteles said, gesturing with his hands for him to say more. Aristoteles liked that Hephaestion, who was as upset as Alexander was about Egypt, was nevertheless participating in class.

"Psyche was motivated by her sisters not to trust her husband. That mistrust led to Psyche breaking the only rule imposed on her," Hephaestion said. "It is just like Orpheus and Eurydice. Orpheus was not allowed to look at Eurydice as he escorted her out of the underworld, but he did and she was banished."

"Relationships require trust," Kallos quickly added. He did not want to be outdone by Hephaestion, and wanted to improve on his earlier response. In a way, he took over Hephaestion's answer. It was a little cheap. Aristoteles allowed it, but Hephaestion did not.

"Of course Psyche had a relationship with her husband before she looked at him," Hephaestion said. "There is more to the story than trust."

"But lack of trust undid their relationship," was all Kallos could muster in response.

"Maybe the focus of the Psyche story should be Eros's clumsiness or the prophecy," Hephaestion added, looking smugly at Alexander, who knew about Hephaestion's dislike of Kallos, and gave Hephaestion a shallow but supportive smile. "Maybe the story is about how relationships are fragile and can't sustain interference, or about beguiling wealth," Hephaestion added, going back to Kallos's initial answer.

Kallos did not respond. It was clear at this point that Hephaestion was toying with Kallos, and Kallos refused to take the bait. He resolved to somehow get even, eventually.

"Maybe," Perseus chimed in, "the story is a little about all of these things. Relationships are complicated. They require trust, have a hard time surviving interference, and are generally fragile. Maybe it also teaches us that harsh rules can set relationships up for failure."

Aristoteles accepted that. "Let's leave it there," he said. Aristoteles felt that some of the myths had several lessons. He did not mind the class thinking about different aspects of it.

Then Aristoteles switched to another myth. "As you know, Jason took the ship *Argo* to Colchis to retrieve a golden fleece guarded by a dragon, so that he would be allowed to marry the daughter of King Pelias of Iolcos. When he got to Colchis, he was asked by the King of Colchis to clear a field and sow it with the teeth of the dragon guarding the golden fleece. Hera and Athena wanted to help Jason, so they got Eros to shoot a golden arrow at Medea, the king's daughter. Medea fell in love with Jason and helped him overcome the dragon. Medea then escaped with Jason on the *Argo*. Medea even killed her own half-brother to delay them being pursued. When Jason returned with the golden fleece, King Pelias did not accept him despite his promises to do so. Medea, still madly in love with Jason, got a poison that she gave to King Pelias's daughter, telling her it was a potion to make King Pelias look younger. When the king died, Jason was blamed. Eventually, Jason and Medea lived in exile in Corinth. There, King Creon, the King of Corinth, wanted Jason to marry his daughter. But Jason ended up alone. Medea left him and even killed their children."

Aristoteles paused. "Medea clearly loved Jason, and he loved her, but there is no happy ending. Why?"

"They truly loved each other, but love is fragile?" Hephaestion responded.

"There is no happy ending," Aristoteles repeated. "Another example: Ariadne gave Theseus a string to help him out of the labyrinth after he killed the Minotaur. Totally in love, they left together. But when Dionysus told Theseus in a dream to leave Ariadne behind, he did.

"And another: Echo, the innocent woman so cursed by only being able to repeat what others said, finally found her love in Narcissus. He rejected her so brutally that she starved herself in a cave. Nemisis, the god of revenge, punished Narcissus by condemning him to stare at his own reflection in a pond. As a result, Narcissus starved as well."

Aristoteles concluded, "None of these end well."

The students tried to disprove Aristoteles.

"Isn't Theseus a hero?" Hephaestion asked. "Isn't the story more about how brave he was?"

"And Narcissus, isn't that about so much more than just the love affair?" Kallos added.

"Yes, and yet, at the end, the love affairs fail," Aristoteles insisted.

"Jason and Medea had a great journey," Marsyus interjected softly. "That is something."

"Andromeda and Perseus, my namesake, found love," Perseus said, and the class quieted down.

Aristoteles smiled. "Go ahead, tell us the story so everyone knows."

"Andromeda's parents boasted about her beauty to the inhabitants of the sea—the Nereids. Nereids believed themselves to be the most beautiful and so they asked Poseidon to send a huge sea monster as punishment. When Andromeda's parents asked how to stop the monster, they were told they could only do so by sacrificing Andromeda to it. They tied her to a rock by the sea, but Perseus saw this and freed her. They got married, had seven sons and two daughters, and loved each other."

When Perseus had chosen a new name, it was unclear what would turn out to be important in a human life. But it was clear that somewhere in that story resided a happiness worth pursuing.

"Thank you," Aristoteles said. "You are right. That one ends well in part because Andromeda's parents did the unthinkable—they offered to sacrifice their daughter. It is an exception that few talk about. Psyche also eventually finds love after much sacrifice on her part. Eros gets his way—he usually does—and marries her. I find it interesting that the one god who causes so much mischief end ups with the beautiful Psyche."

"Maybe he deserved someone less than trustworthy," Perseus said with a knowing smile.

Aristoteles raised an eyebrow at that. "Very well. But let us agree that the myths offer few successful love affairs."

The class became quiet, almost as quiet as when Aristoteles had spoken about Persia, which pleased him. The class seemed discomfited. They wanted to believe in love stories with good endings.

"Does anyone know about Pygmalion and Galatea?" Aristoteles asked.

"I do," Marsyus said quietly when no one else answered. He had forgotten about the story, but it came back to mind. "Pygmalion was a famous sculptor in Cyprus. He was a confirmed bachelor who swore to never fall in love with any women. At one point, Pygmalion made a statue of what he thought a perfect woman would look like, and he fell in love with it. Pygmalion made offerings to the goddess Aphrodite, asking to meet a woman as beautiful as his sculpture. When he went home to his sculpture, he sighed and kissed it. To his surprise, the statue turned into a real woman, Galatea. He married her, and by all accounts they led a happy life."

"So, is that a good example?" Aristoteles asked, in a tone that suggested there was more to the story than the happy ending.

Marysus considered the question. "I am not sure. While it has a happy ending, it may be about man's desire to rule over a woman. He knows what he wants, and will accept only that."

Perseus perked up. This was an interesting and unexpected perspective. "Do you think men are like that?" Perseus asked Marsyus.

"I hope not. Pygmalion had only been with prostitutes when he vowed to be a bachelor. He might not have been able to appreciate what was possible in relationships."

"I think we try to find partners that ascribe to a certain standard," Perseus responded. "We don't love people who are dissimilar to us. It is natural for Pygmalion to have had ideals."

"Yes," Marsyus conceded, "but I am not sure that is right. It seemed like Pygmalion wanted the perfect possession. He was not willing to give and take and appreciate someone for who they are."

Aristoteles was impressed that Marsyus would share his thoughts so openly with a class that might not appreciate such subtlety.

"There is a tension in the story," Aristoteles said. "You either overcome that the person is ideal but not lovable—a statue is not a person—or you change the person by appealing to Aphrodite."

"Any time you form a relationship, don't you change the person?" Perseus asked.

"Yes, but not to suit yourself," Marsyus said. "They are not a possession that you form to suit you."

Perseus was impressed. As Daphne, Perseus had been scared of entering relationships for that very reason: she did not want to be someone's possession, or be limited in what she could do. Marsyus seemed to understand this concern.

"Let's leave it there," Aristoteles said. It was one of the best exchanges he had witnessed the class make so far. He felt proud, the way only a teacher could. Aristoteles wanted to preserve the moment before it strayed into ambiguity. He also wanted to come back to his earlier question. "Again, I ask: Why so few successful love affairs?"

The students debated the questions for a while. All they could agree on was that the stories involving the gods seemed stark, not nuanced.

"It is almost as though the relationships of the gods are like Pygmalion's statue, too perfect or absolute," Marsyus finally said. "There is always some obstacle or absolute principle involved that results in a tragedy."

10. The Fight

One of the first things Leonidas had done when he arrived in Mieza was to separate Alexander and his old friend Hephaestion. The Egyptian invasion emboldened Leonidas to insist on strict discipline, and now Alexander was getting daily lessons on Persian military strategy on top of his lessons with Aristoteles. Left out of these tutoring sessions, Hephaestion had been feeling lonely and vulnerable.

Hephaestion was also still upset about how Kallos had outshone Alexander at the chariot race and then gloated about it. He kept picturing Kallos's smug smirk when he shook hands with Alexander.

Kallos, on the other hand, was jealous of Hephaestion's upbringing and his friendship with Alexander. And he could not forgive Hephaestion for having embarrassed him during the Psyche lecture.

A few days after the lecture, they ran into each other near the nymphaeum.

"How about that race?" Kallos started, still boasting about his victory. He straightened his back and looked threateningly at Hephaestion.

"What race?" Hephaestion asked, throwing back his shoulders and staring at Kallos.

"Bucephalus is beatable after all," Kallos said, ignoring Hephaestion's feigned oblivion and naming the horse instead of its rider. In a way, this was less offensive, but Hephaestion saw it as a claim that Alexander had an advantage in the race which Kallos had overcome—like he had beaten Alexander by a wide margin.

"What is your problem?" Hephaestion sneered, taking a step closer to Kallos. Kallos was a little taller than Hephaestion and more muscular, not by a lot, but enough. Hephaestion was unsure about the threatening posture he was taking but considered it an act of bravery. He would stand up to Kallos.

"What is *your* problem?" Kallos said, raising his voice, standing up for himself.

The two glared at each other. Hephaestion knew he would probably not win a fight with Kallos, and Kallos was concerned that winning it would not be smart. Yet they both resolved to be heroes, to fight for whatever they felt they were standing up for.

Hephaestion thought about how best to insult Kallos further. Being a wrestler himself, he knew Kallos probably suffered from the idiotic stereotype that athletes can't be academics—promulgated by people who were neither. He would not stoop to that. He would mock Kallos where it hurt him most.

"What are you doing here anyway?" Hephaestion said. "Looking for help with the lectures? Come to learn more about Psyche?"

Kallos knew how to respond. "Ready to come out from behind Alexander's shadow? Where is he, anyway? Do you even know who you are without him?"

Hephaestion threw the first punch. It hit Kallos on his shoulder, knocking him back. He almost fell but did not. The surprise on Kallos's face was something Hephaestion would not forget for a long time.

At that moment, Hephaestion crossed the threshold to something he was bound to regret.

As Kallos stumbled, he smiled. He had gotten to Hephaestion, and now it was time for him to return the favor. He was glad Hephaestion had been first to cross the line.

He pushed Hephaestion to the ground. Hephaestion got up, and the two went back and forth for a while. Soon, they both began to fear that they had embarked on a battle that might not end, but had to somehow.

Hephaestion threw another punch. This one hit Kallos on his right cheek, and it would leave a mark. At least, if or when he lost, it would be clear that he put up a good fight.

Kallos ran toward Hephaestion, grabbing him by his waist and pushing him to the ground. Then he sat on top of him and punched Hephaestion's chest. "You bastard!" Kallos yelled.

Hephaestion squirmed underneath Kallos trying get free, but to no avail. Kallos continued to throw punches.

"What are you doing?" Perseus yelled, running up with Phaenon. Perseus grabbed Kallos and pulled him off Hephaestion, while Phaenon helped Hephaestion up and stood between the two of them.

"Stop it," Perseus yelled at Kallos, while Phaenon gave Hephaestion a look of disapproval that told him he should know better.

Perseus and Phaenon's presence gave Kallos and Hephaestion the excuse they needed to stop the fight. Now they both could walk away with some pride.

They were covered in mud. Phaenon could not help but think that they looked like a pair of boars that had dug up a field. Phaenon knew fights were not accepted in Athenian schools. Ever since Athens had lost its empire to the Spartans, they had taken what Phaenon believed to be exaggerated refuge in their mores, which strictly required intellectual over physical jousting. A physical fight was sure to result in expulsion.

"This is not over," Kallos yelled, looking back at Hephaestion as Perseus escorted him away. It was a ridiculous, brutish thing to say, and Kallos snorted slightly at himself.

Let's hope it is, Phaenon thought. He didn't want to see either boy expelled.

Hephaestion called back, "Any time." Then he flung his hair out of his face, straightened out, and walked away with Phaenon.

Perseus wondered whether the fight could be considered both courageous and juvenile. If the fight had been between the gods, the answer would be clear.

11. Second Set of Games

"Well, that was fun to watch," Zeus said sarcastically .

"They fight over nothing," Hera said dismissively. "Defending insecurities they devise for themselves."

"I am not sure the Apollo–Daphne drama has more meaning," Zeus said.

"Perhaps not. Regardless, we are about to get closer to finding out who Apollo is. Phaenon is running against Perseus, and Krasi is playing the loser in Petteia. Both real contenders, Krasi with his charm and joy, and Phaenon with his hard work and bright future. Interesting choices."

"I wish it had been Kallos," Zeus confessed with a sigh. He admired Kallos's physical strength and command of a chariot. A simple, straightforward choice.

"Krasi and Phaenon would both be more sophisticated choices," Hera retorted.

"We still don't know whether Apollo can ever overcome the arrows."

"One thing at a time," Hera said, "Personally, I want to see how attuned Apollo is to Daphne's needs. You should be proud of him if he chose wisely."

It was early in the morning, and Marsyus appeared at the farmhouse where Perseus was staying.

Perseus was still inside, fretting over the race. *I have not trained for this*, Perseus thought. *After all, I was a tree before I came here.* Then Perseus remembered all the running in the forest before that, particularly the running away from Apollo.

Maybe it will come back to me, Perseus thought, chuckling, and went outside.

Marsyus was waiting.

"I am surprised to see you," Perseus said.

"I want to support you in this. You were there to cheer for me."

"Well thank you, I am glad you are here. I need some support. I am not sure I am up for the race," Perseus said.

"You can beat him if you want," Marsyus said eagerly. "You are younger. It will come down to strategy. Remember, if you go out too strong at the beginning of the race, you will exhaust yourself and slow down too much at the end." Marsyus suspected that Perseus knew this, but wanted to make sure.

Perseus perked up. A desire to win, if only for Marsyus, started to take over.

"I really appreciate your support," Perseus said.

Since Perseus seemed open to advice, Marsyus went on. "Run so you are only slightly uncomfortable for the first half of the race. Don't keep up with Phaenon if you can't. He may be exhausting himself. Then push as hard as you can for the second half. It has to be all you; not even the gods will help."

The venue for the footrace was the same as the path for the chariot race between Kallos and Alexander. When Perseus and Marsyus arrived, Aristoteles, Theophrastus, and all the other students were already there.

Phaenon approached Perseus in a relaxed and casual manner.

"I hope we have a good race," Phaenon said in his usual aristocratic way, stretching out his hand.

Perseus got the sense that Phaenon was playing up his sportsmanship, as though the race were more about him proving that he had the right manner as opposed the physical strength.

"The gods like a good race. May the best person win," Perseus said, feeling like outdoing Phaenon's aloofness, and winking at the sky.

"Yes, we do," Zeus said, chuckling, and moved to the edge of his throne.

Hera also moved to the edge of her throne and smiled at Zeus. She wanted to seize the chance to bond with Zeus. It had been a long time since they had both been passionate about the same thing. They looked like fans excited about the first match of a season.

Aristoteles took his time to start the race. Foot races were an important tradition in Athens, a quintessential human sport. He enjoyed their simplicity. Aristoteles stood at the sideline and inquired if both runners were ready. He raised his right arm. When both runners nodded confidently, Aristoteles put on a cheerful smile and lowered his arm to signal them to start.

Phaenon forced himself to push hard, and when he disappeared behind the hill, he was well ahead of Perseus. He took pride in being ahead and smiled, but quickly realized he needed his cheeks to force air into his lungs. He was starting to run out of breath. He still had energy, but the sudden onset of running out of breath scared him. Phaenon slowed down.

When the two appeared again from behind the hill, Phaenon was still in front, but Perseus had made up most of the distance between them.

Perseus started to put a push on, forcing arms and legs into a short, powerful and quick rhythm. It was a continuous smooth motion unimpeded by any negative thoughts. Perseus felt no pain and even forgot about the race—just enjoying the continuous smooth movement of gliding over the path.

Perseus overtook Phaenon.

When they came to the final stretch of the race, Phaenon realized that he did not need to be scared about running out of breath or finishing anymore. He confidently picked up his speed, impeded only by the pain in his lungs. He pulled ahead of Perseus.

Perseus, still overtaken by the sheer joy of the run, took stronger strides while retaining a smooth rhythm, sped up, and caught Phaenon.

The crowd cheered when they approached the finish line, even Aristoteles. They were cheering for both runners, not caring who won. The crowd was impressed how fast both were running, and took pleasure in what was possible.

At the end, Perseus was not able to recapture the lead from Phaenon. But it did not matter. Both runners were elated and hugged and congratulated each other. It was a sight to behold. They were living in the moment.

"A great race," Aristoteles said cheerfully. "I am sure the gods were impressed." He placed the laurel wreath on Phaenon.

Zeus and Hera were not that impressed. They had no interest in the joy of the race. Their concern was with who won.

"I suppose you are disappointed," Zeus said to Hera. "Admit it, you were rooting for Phaenon to be Apollo's choice— the hard-working man with a future."

"Over Krasi, maybe. Krasi is too much into having fun," Hera said, even though she liked how Krasi did not get himself embroiled in things.

Zeus smiled. How can one have too much fun?

"Well, let's see if it is Krasi," Zeus said consoling Hera in a way.

Since Perseus had lost, he was the one who had to play Krasi in Pettiea after the race.

"Just keep up your concentration," Marsyus said to Perseus as they walked to a table that had been set up next to the racetrack. Krasi was already sitting there with his usual big smile.

"That's not easy with Krasi," Perseus responded. "He loves the world, and it loves him."

"You can do it," Marsyus said. "Just pretend he is the Minotaur."

"I appreciate all your support, Adriadne!" Perseus joked.

Perseus sat down on the bench opposite Krasi. Perseus couldn't help liking him.

"I am glad it is you," Krasi said. "I am not sure I wanted to play the aristocrat. Do you care who starts?"

The game had one larger main piece, a variation of Petteia that was becoming popular—encircling it on all four sides meant you immediately won the game.

"The rules require us to throw a die for it," Perseus said. "Let's stick to the rules."

Krasi smiled, produced a die, and threw a six. Perseus threw a four.

Krasi chose the white pieces and started placing them.

"I am still surprised you got Aristoteles to agree to play this game," Perseus said.

"It's more fun than whipping horses or running races, you must agree," Krasi said.

Perseus smiled. Then both players concentrated on the game.

Perseus and Krasi furiously moved their pieces around trying to box in the pieces of the other. It went back and forth but never got close. None could capture the other.

After a while, Aristoteles called the first game a draw.

Perseus and Krasi finished setting up their pieces and started moving them furiously around the board again. Aristoteles and the students stepped back from the table a little. They gave up anticipating what each player would do. It was exhausting to watch.

At one point, when Krasi was sure only Perseus could hear him, he whispered, "You know, I am ready for something not in the moment."

It stunned Perseus. "Oh? Well . . . there is no stopping the successes you could achieve."

Perseus thought, *With his charm, Krasi could take over the world if he cared to.*

Both moved some pieces.

Perseus couldn't fathom Krasi's meaning. Was this a throwback to the party? Why was he whispering?

It did not take long for Krasi to encircle Perseus' pieces and win.

"You distracted me on purpose!" Perseus said when he lost.

Krasi smiled. "It is all fair in this game."

Perseus was upset. "You are like one of those pieces on the board. Always reacting to the moment, but never able to do anything lasting."

Krasi did not know what to say. He had not been able to resist winning even if it would cost him Perseus's friendship. And that was exactly what had upset Perseus.

Aristoteles overhead this and quickly crowned Krasi the winner. It was a somber moment.

Perseus left Krasi standing alone with his laurel wreath.

"Well, Krasi is out," Zeus said, pleased that Hera would not be upset about Apollo's choice.

"The good-looking one is out, the one who lives in his future is out, and the one that lives in the present is out," Hera said to Zeus. "So Apollo is either Hephaestion or Marsyus."

"Whoever it is, this may still end up like Torin and Keelycael," Zeus reminded her.

Part III

1. The Final Game—Two Poems

About a week passed when it was time for the final competition. Aristoteles wanted to wrap up the competitions, and he was especially looking forward to the poetry part. Poetry was important to Athenian culture, but it did not fit into his lectures. Poetry expressed feelings and emotions, and Aristoteles was trying to portray a rational world.

Alexander and Hephaestion were so passionate about poetry that they read it in their free time—both epic and tragic. It bonded them. They had in fact read poems in Mieza until Leonidas appeared and forbade it, being focused, as always, on military matters. Fortunately, Leonidas had been asked only to instruct Alexander on Egypt, and left when that was done.

The students gathered outside of the nymphaeum. The benches had been moved outside and arranged in a half circle to put the speaker more in the center of things. Aristoteles wanted this to be a performance, not a lecture.

Hephaestion was the first to recite his poem. He had worked hard on it. After wanting it to be part of the competition, he could not fail. He had gone through many potential subjects and drafts. Hephaestion had refused to share it with Alexander in advance, even when Alexander had insisted. Hephaestion only wanted to share it when it was done. Now that it was finished, he was sure it would please Alexander.

"My poem is about Patroclus, the hero and best friend of Achilles in the *Iliad*." Hephaestion said. He composed himself and looked at Alexander as he recited his poem.

Patroclus

In the morning, I stand in an open field
I note the breeze the gods revealed

In the morning, I see the sun rise tall
I feel the embrace that unites us all

You know there is a greater good
Yearning to protect it as we should

You fight in the field next to me
Joining together to shield destiny

This is not about us anymore
We are fighting a united war

This is what makes us complete
We find purpose even in defeat

In the evening, we lie in the battlefield
Grasping at what is about to yield

In the evening, the sun shows sincerity
Uniting us with pride for eternity

At first there was a moment of silence, then the students broke out in smiles and cheers. They liked the heroism in the poem, and they were impressed with how Hephaestion had captured what they liked about the *Illiad.*

The poem also provided an outlet for the anxiety everyone still felt about the Persians. The students had not spoken about it lately. They'd had no news, and discussions always ended in the same place—fear of the unknown. It was best to ignore the matter and focus on the strength of the empire. The poem helped with that. With such heroism among them, surely Macedonia could not be beaten. It also brought back memories of simpler times when the boys focused on heroes in the *Illiad.*

"Inspiring," Alexander declared, even though it was not really his place.

Aristoteles nodded once approvingly when the class looked at him. Then he announced in a contemplative tone, "May you all become Patroclus." He did not say "and may the gods help you," even though he was thinking it. He thought exaggerated heroism dangerous—always had.

Hephaestion was a tough act to follow. Once again, Marsyus was perceived as the underdog, presumed to have lost before he started.

"I can't wait to hear your poem," Perseus said kindly to Marsyus. "I am sure it will impress everyone."

"Thank you," Marsyus said softly. "I will be content if you like it."

Then he straightened out and turned to the class. "My poem is about what we yearn for even when there is no winning," Marsyus declared.

Imprisoned Inside a Statue

In your youth you ran in forests found
Only restraints did you confound
I was still a boulder lying around
Admiring from afar without a sound

I became a statue to gain attention
And studied and feigned some comprehension
I restrained myself with the best intention
Yet you disregarded my reinvention

I am imprisoned in that statue of perfection
Unable to reveal myself or my deception
I am suffering until you allow a love connection
Undo my confinement, show me affection

Let's give ourselves love uncontained
Let's condemn all thoughts of restraint

Again, there was a moment of silence, but it lingered.

"Another great poem," Aristoteles finally declared. This time he wondered where the feelings of inadequacies Marsyus expressed in the poem had come from. *No fulfilled person could write such a poem*, he thought.

When Aristoteles had first prepared for his lectures in Mieza, he'd told Theophrastus that young pupils prefer heroic stories. Marsyus was much further along. Aristoteles wondered if the other pupils had matured as well. But the only one who appeared moved was Perseus.

Perseus was startled by the way the opening of the poem described Apollo. But of course, Perseus did not know that Apollo was there, and so did not consider that Marsyus was him.

Perseus was caught up in the universality of the poem. The poem reflected Perseus's own feelings, and Perseus was sure others felt the same about it. The person trapped in the statue exhibiting perfection to attract a suitor, but wanting to get out and reveal the true self. The statue was in a suspenseful state until, like Pygmalion's statue, it was kissed and appreciated fully. Then and only then did Galatea come to life, and then and only then did Pygmalion come to life. Marsyus had written the poem from Galatea's perspective. That was also interesting.

Perseus then considered the poem from Daphne's perspective. *Confined in a tree, I suffered like a statue—forced to observe and not allowed to live. Being here, learning with the future leaders of Macedonia has given me some life. The logical universe taught by Aristoteles is intriguing, but it is not enough. To have someone to share a life with, that would be true liberation. Marsyus captured this so perfectly. Life without love is like being a statue, confined to exhibiting unhuman perfection.*

Tears started rolling down Perseus's face. *I am still confined. When will I be liberated? When will I finally have feelings about someone? When will someone finally have feelings for me?*

The class noticed that Perseus was upset but said nothing, creating a silence that compounded the difficulty of ignoring Perseus. Yet, the class continued to show compassion, pretending not to notice Perseus's state.

Marsyus was encouraged. The poem had had its intended effect. It had moved Perseus, without the unnecessary and risky revelation that he was Apollo. That could wait until Daphne was also willing to reveal her past.

Alexander, fearing that Aristoteles or the class might support Marsyus's poem given Perseus' reaction, interrupted the silence. "Our empire will grow with soldiers like Patroclus." Then he started applauding, first slowly and then more vehemently, hoping others would join.

Phaenon joined immediately, knowing it was the prudent thing to do. Marsyus's poem had resonated somewhat with him, but he would always support Alexander. He did think both poems were good, certainly better than the down-to-earth Hesiod poems Leviat told him she liked.

Kallos also applauded. He had been genuinely moved and caught up in Hephaestion's poem. It had validated the idea that the military had a purpose, in his mind. It made you part of something important. Even if you were injured or killed, at least you stood for something and had a glorious life. You would be admired for what you did. Kallos applauded so loudly that Hephaestion noticed and smiled, and a reconciliation was set in motion. While Kallos could not replace Hephaestion as Alexander's best friend, especially after a poem like that, he could become a friend to them both.

Aristoteles was not sure which poem should be the winner of the competition. Hephaestion's had inspired the class, and he deserved recognition. Hephaestion generally avoided being recognized for his achievements, not wanting to upstage Alexander. Declaring Hephaestion the winner for something Alexander appreciated was the right thing to do. However, Marsyus's poem had such depth and maturity. Even if only Perseus had noticed this, the rest of the class eventually might, if they reflected on it. What better way was there to cause the class to reflect than to declare Marsyus the winner?

Aristoteles surprised the class by saying he would wait to crown the winner. He wanted them to understand that both poems were worthy of applause.

The gods liked Marsyus's poem best. To be fair, they were the only ones who realized who and what the poem was for. Zeus in particular was moved by the strength of emotions Marsyus showed in the poem. He was overtaken by paternal pride.

"Apollo chose someone who understands and is capable of love," Zeus thought.

Zeus could not help but think about the many forms he himself had taken to be loved, and the liberation that had come from being accepted. Besides seducing Leda as a swan and Europa as a bull (which Aristoteles had fretted over), he had also seduced Kallisto, a princess of Arkadia, in the form of the goddess Artemis; Alkmene, a lady of Thebes, by taking the form of her husband; and Eurymedousa, a princess of Phthiotis, in the form of an ant. Zeus was getting emotional thinking about the special feeling he always got when, at least for a moment, he was loved despite human imperfections.

"Apollo captured this in his poem so well," Zeus thought, when Hera interrupted.

"Hephaestion and Alexander are enthralled with each other. They have not broken any of our rules and have been loyal to each other. We should have known all along that Apollo could not have chosen Hephaestion. Now that we know Apollo chose Marsyus, Aristoteles must crown Hephaestion. There is no other alternative."

"I agree," Zeus said, composing himself amid the pride and compassion he felt for his son. "Marsyus had the better poem, but Hephaestion must be the winner."

Then Zeus thought about the challenges ahead. Daphne still had the lead arrow, after all.

In fact, he was not at all sure which poem was the cry to battle and which was the love poem.

2. The Boar Hunt

With the competitions finished, Aristoteles let Alexander organize a boar hunt. Boars were known to be particularly large and strong in the forests around Mieza. It was a special treat, though it was rather too early in the season. Many boars were still with their younglings.

The hunt involved riding on horseback until a boar was found, and after wearing it out in a chase, tracking it by foot until it stood to fight. Then the skilled hunter would kill the boar with a spear. The trick was to get close enough to the boar while not being charged by it.

It was a gloomy summer morning with the weather threatening to cut the hunt short. The gray sky blended all the colors of the forest into a uniform green. A gray mist hid mosquitoes that were encouraged by the moisture. The hunt would be difficult and potentially unpleasant, but the students were undeterred.

The hunt was organized into three groups. Aristoteles was riding with Alexander and Hephaestion; Theophrastus was riding with Marsyus and Perseus; the last group was Phaenon, Kallos, and Krasi. They arrived first at the gathering spot and were the most eager to succeed. When the others arrived, they raced ahead, trying to complete a successful hunt before the weather changed.

"Where do you think our chances are best?" Hephaestion asked Alexander while they were getting ready.

"Closer to the river," Alexander answered. "Boars like the mud on the riverbank."

Aristoteles was unfamiliar with hunts, particularly in this region. He followed Alexander and Hephaestion down a path to the river.

Along the way, they saw small wildlife and even some deer. They saw boar tracks, but no boar. When they got to the river, they rode down the bank, intermittently entering the water where there was no beach. The horses' hooves beat the river with abandon, making a loud thrashing sound, splashing in every direction. Alexander and Hephaestion enjoyed that, but it was sure to scare away any boar that might be near.

Theophrastus, Marsyus, and Perseus were a reluctant hunting group and started late. Theophrastus did not want to kill any animals. He was riding along only for show. Marsyus was more interested in pursuing Perseus. Only Perseus was interested in the hunt.

"Let's head to some of the wetlands," Marsyus suggested, wanting to avoid the river. Marsyus thought the river was special and wanted to experience it with Perseus another time. When the time was right. When they were ready.

The group slowly trotted off into the forest. In places, the thicket that was tough to pass through, and they were moving slowly.

"We may not be able to see boar in this underbrush," Marsyus commented.

"Yes, but they can't see us either," Perseus said. "They'll become active when we get close. Trust me. Then we will notice them."

"Have you hunted a lot?" Marsyus asked.

"I have witnessed a lot of hunts. But I am not an expert. I am not much good with a spear if it comes to that."

Marsyus saw humor in how deviously honest Perseus was being and decided to push this further.

"How about a bow and arrow? Are you good with those?" Marsyus asked.

"Pretty good, actually," Perseus answered.

Marsyus smiled to himself. *That's my Daphne*, he thought, *doesn't want to tell a lie.*

"We will be at the wetlands soon," Theophrastus said from behind. "Marsyus and I have been there before to collect plants."

When they arrived, there was no time for plants: several boars were congregated in an area filled with lush grass and flowers. The boars were covered in mud. Some were chewing on something, presumably roots and not flowers, while others were playing and still digging. The boars looked at the approaching riders as though they owned the land and stood their ground.

"Let's stop and approach slowly," Perseus whispered.

Marsyus and Theophrastus pulled on their reins.

"Is it a family? This is dangerous," Marsyus said.

"Yes, with some small males," Perseus answered.

The boar family reminded Marsyus of the family he as Apollo observed with Daphne, when they first met. Marsyus wondered if Perseus would notice the similarity, but Perseus was too caught up in the moment. It was part of Perseus's subtle change since becoming a human, the desire to prove oneself as opposed to observe. Marsyus noticed it.

Eventually, the group of boars got spooked and started running, except for an older female. She started charging. She lowered her tusks, dug in her hind legs, and catapulted toward Perseus and Marsyus, whose horses were standing next to each other. She grunted loudly and dirt flew as she charged. Horses and even their riders had been killed this way. There was no stopping an angry sow, and this one was particularly angry, given that there were young ones around.

As the sow was charging, Perseus and Marsyus froze, not knowing what to do. They made a perfect target and there was not much time. The sow was already halfway toward them, and Marsyus thought about summoning help from the gods, who could, of course, figure out all sorts of ways to stop the charging animal that was only seconds away.

"Hold," Perseus yelled to Marsyus, interrupting his thoughts. "When she is about three seconds aways, whip your horse and go to the right of her. I will go to the left and give her room so she can't hook your horse."

Marsyus's heart was pumping. If he summoned the gods, it would reveal who he was. Wasn't risk also part of the experience? Wasn't life about risks? Wasn't he supposed to take chances?

"Now," Perseus yelled. They both darted forward with their horses. The sow did not have time to change direction. She swung her head right and left, trying to hook one of the horses' legs with her tusks as they darted past her. But Perseus and Marsyus had left enough room, and they escaped her rampage.

"Keep going, let's get away from here!" Perseus yelled, smiling at Marsyus with pure joy. Danger overcome—it was thrilling. Perseus and Marsyus could not help but laugh as they continued to ride.

"Let's follow the males," Perseus yelled, referring to two young males that had split from the group before the female boar charged.

Theophrastus followed from a distance. Staying well away from the commotion had served him well.

"Let's follow that one," Perseus screamed and picked up his pace. Marsyus was having a hard time keeping up, as was Theophrastus, who fell farther behind.

A few times the young boar they were chasing stopped in thicket, but Perseus found him every time and chased him up again. They went up and down hills, not keeping to any of the cleared paths. They even crossed some streams as they continued the chase. Eventually, the boar became tired and stood his ground.

"This is it," Perseus said, glad the chase was over. Now it was time to finish the hunt. Perseus waited until Marsyus caught up and then they both dismounted, took their spears and approached the animal.

Theophrastus rode up slowly and watched the two from his horse. He did not dismount.

"A beautiful animal," Perseus said, and raised a spear.

"Yes," Marsyus responded. "What shall we do?"

The question surprised Perseus. They were meant to kill the animal, or at least try to.

Perseus took a step back and looked at Marsyus, spear still up.

"What do you mean? We kill it," Perseus said quietly but forcefully, trying to make a point while not spooking the boar.

"The chase was enjoyable. The kill usually isn't," Marsyus said.

Perseus was surprised but lowered the spear a little annoyed at Marsyus. If they did not kill the animal the other students would laugh at them.

"Theophrastus doesn't want the boar killed. We can pretend we didn't because of him," Marsyus said.

Marsyus was reminiscing about the innocent times with Daphne when they'd observed boars in the forest. How could they now kill one? Perseus did not make the connection but nevertheless sensed that it would seriously upset Marsyus to kill the boar.

"The boar is rather young," Perseus said with a smile, and shrugged. The movement spooked the boar, who turned his head and ran away.

Perseus and Marsyus walked back to their horses, smiling at Theophrastus as though they had done something to please him. Theophrastus tried not to smile back to avoid having his expression be misinterpreted as having somehow scored a victory. He looked to the ground.

"You really don't care what the others think?" Perseus asked Marsyus.

"It is not why I came here," Marsyus responded, with some duplicitous honesty of his own.

"I admire your independence, Marsyus," Perseus said, still too focused on the hunt to note the playful tone in Marsyus's answer.

"Don't get me wrong, I do care what you think, and about Theophrastus. I just don't care about impressing Alexander," Marsyus responded.

Perseus did not know how to respond.

They started riding back. Perseus thought about agreeing on an exact story about the hunt with Marsyus, not sure what Marsyus would say, but decided it was more important to show Marsyus some trust.

When they got back to where they'd started, Aristoteles, Alexander, and Hephaestion were already there, having cut their hunt short. Phaenon, Kallos, and Krasi had also just arrived. They had been successful in their hunt, but no one really took notice.

The clouds had cleared without rain, and the forest was back in full splendor. The afternoon sun lit parts of the forest and cast dark shadows in others. A calm settled, enhanced by the warm sun and a subtle breeze.

The servants distributed glasses of wine.

"Not watered down," Alexander said to Aristoteles as he raised a glass.

"Yes, one must respect the local customs." Aristoteles raised his glass.

The calm was disturbed when Kallos, in his usual bluster brought up Persia. He was seriously thinking about joining the army and wanted to talk about the strength the Persians were building and his commitment.

Alexander looked to the ground, concerned about the problem he would eventually have to deal with. He appreciated Kallos's enthusiasm and patriotism, but did not want to talk about Persia. "We will beat them," Alexander finally said, raising his glass in aspiration, and then with a smile to Theophrastus, "and we will send you back those Persian plants you've been wondering about."

Theophrastus smiled and toasted back. "I am sure you will," he said.

They fell silent again, and sat there enjoying the forest and the wine. It was the last time they spoke about Persia.

"I almost forgot," Aristoteles said after a while. He felt enough time had passed for him to have made the point about the poetry competition not having a clear winner. His decision had also been delayed by consideration of the fight between Hephaestion and Kallos, which he eventually heard about. At the end, he decided to ignore the fight along with the fact that Marsyus' poem deserved to win. It was more important for all the students to feel appreciated in their opinion than to stick to principles. The same was true about the fight. Sometimes Athenian mores had to be compromised.

"Hephaestion is the winner of the poetry competition," Aristoteles said. He walked to his horse and got the laurel wreath.

"For a heroic poem. Well done," Aristoteles said and placed the laurel wreath on Hephaestion, who did not even have time to get up. Hephaestion, surprised and unsure he should have won, accepted the wreath with a reluctant smile.

It was a relaxing afternoon, and being able to have a good time even after a generally unsuccessful hunt made Aristoteles feel closer to the students. It was more about the company than anything else. Aristoteles did not have many opportunities like this.

Marsyus, on the other hand, was far from relaxed. He was not making any progress with Perseus.

"I am glad you agreed not to kill the boar," Marsyus said to Perseus, trying to not let the hunt go to waste.

"How about that charging boar?" Perseus said quietly, looking at the ground.

They'd escaped danger, but there was nothing to discuss. It was what it was—an obvious choice and a successful outcome.

Marsyus thought the decision to let the male boar go was more interesting—not so obvious.

"Just like with Pygmalion, you don't need to possess everything you like," Marsyus said.

Perseus felt that the comment was awkward and did not respond. It was the lead arrow talking.

3. Pan Painting

The next day, the lecture was held at Alexander's house. Finally they would learn why Theophrastus had asked Alexander to bring the painting of Pan with him to Mieza.

The painting was by the Greek artist Zeuxis. It was famous in Macedonia. It had been commissioned by Archelaus I, Alexander's grandfather to adorn the new palace when it was built in Pella. There were few pieces of art in the palace. Instead much attention had been given to its architecture, which emulated a Greek temple, and to its well organized gardens, with rows of flowers. The gardens were to provide serenity to leaders who shunned seeking it, like they shunned the painting. They were too ambitious. Alexander's father, King Philip, did not even notice that the painting had been taken to Mieza.

For the class, Alexander had the painting put on an easel in the center of the room where he'd held his first party. The students were to copy the painting as best they could. When they arrived, they found that the painting had been covered with a cloth.

Theophrastus led the lecture. "Zeuxis was one of the greatest painters of his time. It is said that he had a painting contest with his rival, Parrhasius. During it, Zeuxis painted grapes. Birds pecked at the painting when it was unveiled. It was that real. Parrhasius then asked Zeuxis to pull at a curtain to unveil his painting. When he did, Zeuxis discovered that the curtain was in the painting. Zeuxis deceived the birds, but Parrhasius deceived Zeuxis, the artist, and was considered the winner. Now, I am not sure if the story is true, but Zeuxis is a great artist as you will see."

Theophrastus walked over to the painting to pull the cloth away. "I am assured that the cloth is not in the painting," Theophrastus joked, and then revealed it.

The class gasped at the realism with which Zeuxis depicted the god of the wild, shepherds and flocks, and rustic music—and, of course, the companion of all too many nymphs. Pan had the hindquarters, legs, and horns of a goat attached to a human body and head wearing a floral wreath. He looked like a satyr.

"Pan is real. He defies classification. He is half animal and half human," Theophrastus said, and chuckled.

So that the students could learn from each other, Theophrastus asked them to pair up.

"After you choose a partner, you need to decide how to work together in copying the painting," Theophrastus said. He considered the exercise to be as much about working together as it was about art. It was a novel approach that Aristoteles was not sure he liked.

Alexander, of course, chose Hephaestion, and Marsyus quickly chose Perseus. That left Kallos, Krasi, and Phaenon, who were used to being a team from the hunt.

Alexander and Hephaestion decided to start painting Pan together from the bottom up. They started jointly painting his hoofs.

"That way we will be used to working together when we get to the head, the toughest part," Alexander said.

"And the hands—they are as hard as the face," Hephaestion added.

Kallos, Krasi, and Phaenon decided to divide Pan into three parts. Kallos was to paint the powerful hindquarters, Krasi the torso, and Phaenon the head.

Marsyus and Perseus came up with a third strategy. "I think we should first both paint an outline and decide which one to fill in," Marsyus suggested. "That way we are sure that the figure is in proportion before we get to the detail."

Perseus agreed, and they both quickly sketched outlines of Pan.

"Yours is great," Marsyus said to Perseus.

"So is yours. I am not sure it matters whose we take."

They took Perseus' outline and painstakingly completed all the details of the painting—working together at each part. They complimented each other as they went along. Having agreed on the whole, they easily agreed on the parts. They finished quickly.

Perseus frowned. "The horns are too big."

Marsyus was surprised how worried Perseus was about getting the painting just right. It showed vulnerability, and Marsyus was surprised to find he liked it.

"I am not sure it matters," Marsyus said. "Who knows how big they really were, right? At least they are both too big."

"Maybe bigger is good," Perseus said, smiling.

Then they stepped back and admired what they had done. They were happy with it.

Theophrastus was impressed.

"You work well together," he said. "It is a great painting. We have to make sure it is not mistaken for the original," Theophrastus joked, winking at them.

Theophrastus examined Alexander and Hephaestion's painting. It was a mixture of two styles that created a third. Alexander's lines were precise and thin, painted meticulously with a small brush. Hephaestion's lines were abstract and broad, painted quickly with large strokes. The combination of styles gave their painting a unique abstract look.

"Very artistic," Theophrastus said.

Alexander and Hephaestion were happy. It was the first time that Hephaestion had undertaken something with Alexander that made him feel like an equal. No one was better or worse, no one was meant to be. Alexander felt the same; painting was liberating in that regard.

Kallos watched as Alexander and Hephaestion looked proudly at their painting together. It confirmed what he'd thought after Hephaestion's poem recitation. If he wanted to befriend Alexander, he would have to form a bond with Hephaestion.

Kallos, Krasi, and Phaenon did not quite manage a real collaboration. Each of the three parts, the head, the torso, and the hindquarters, were painted differently. It showed that Pan was part human and part animal, but in an unrealistic, awkward way. The human parts did not blend with the animal parts since different painters had painted them. Kallos was not proud of it and walked away. "Great work," Kallos said genuinely to Alexander and Hephaestion when he saw theirs.

"Thank you," Alexander said, and Hephaestion nodded.

Theophrastus liked Alexander and Hephaestion's painting best. It was the most artistic. However, the most realistic copy, which after all was the assignment, was the painting by Perseus and Marsyus. Theophrastus recognized them in front of the class.

"Perseus and Marsyus did the best job copying the painting," Theophrastus said. "But now I want you to tell me whether Pan seems more like a human or an animal in the painting."

All agreed that Pan looked more like a human with animal parts than the other way around. Perseus was the one to say so, but the other students nodded.

"Does anyone know why?" Theophrastus asked.

Neither Perseus nor the rest of the class had any idea.

"Notice that Pan in the painting is wearing a wreath adorned with beautiful little flowers in a variety of colors, on his grotesque head. He has a weakness. He cares about how he looks. This is reinforced by the disturbed look on his face. It is as though he knows that the viewer will be repulsed by his looks despite the flowers. That weakness, that caring ultimately makes him appear human."

The students liked this. It was a great way to end class.

Marsyus clapped Perseus on the shoulder as they left. "We did it! It was a great collaboration."

"I am glad we won, though painting seems a strange activity for competition." Perseus said. "It seems like the sort of thing you should just enjoy."

"I agree," Marsyus said, wishing he had thought of that. He was happy that Perseus' competitiveness had boundaries.

"Do you want to keep the painting?" Perseus asked Marsyus.

"No, I don't need to own it," Marsyus said, wanting to say more, that the process of painting was enough. The experience of creating the painting mattered more than its possession. That should have appealed to Daphne, but he had said something similar after the boar hunt and it fell flat.

Perseus thought that even the simple comment about not needing to own the painting was awkward.

"Fascinating creature, that Pan," Perseus said. "I have to study up on his stories some time." Perseus waved goodbye and left.

Marsyus knew that Perseus was familiar with Pan—Daphne could have even met him, since Daphne and Pan both liked to roam the forests. Perseus was again deflecting his advances.

4. Apollo's Appeal

Marsyus had made several attempts to get closer to Perseus. He had been considerate and careful not to push too hard. *Yet every time we find common ground, I am rejected.* He'd thought he was making progress at the sporting competitions when they supported each other. He'd thought the Pygmalion lecture, the boar hunt, and the painting should have brought them closer, but nothing seemed to work.

It felt to Marsyus like it was a continuation of the times he'd chased Daphne as Apollo. His continued declaration of love back then might have put Daphne off, but he was not doing that now. He was being wiser and more subtle in his pursuit, catering to Daphne and not just declaring his love, but it was not working. He remained oblivious to the lead arrow.

Marsyus felt that he had no option but to return to Mount Olympus to seek advice and help from his father, Zeus. He preferred not to. It had risks. He recalled the many stories of gods faltering and making things worse. They had even discussed one of them at length in Aristoteles's class—the tragic history of King Laius and his son Oedipus. If the gods had not issued a prophecy, much could have been avoided.

Moreover, Zeus in particular did not have a good history of dealing with mortals. It was a well-known fact that even though he changed forms for them, at the end he forced himself onto many of the women he pursued. This even included Hera, for whom he had changed himself into a little bird before taking advantage of her. Apollo was not sure he should take advice from such a person. What would he know about love? What would he recommend? Ultimately, though, he felt he had no other option and went to consult his father, the god of gods.

Apollo approached Zeus and Hera in their white robes sitting on their white thrones surrounded by white marble. He had not been there for a while and his eyes hurt from the brightness. He had to walk slowly to let them adjust.

Apollo could see the flame in the fire pit but only when he walked right by it. He also noticed his laurel wreath, which he had left on his seat.

He stood in front of Zeus' throne, not between Zeus' and Hera's. Hera would not be his ally; he was appealing to his father. His shoulders slumped and he was not his usual assertive self.

"I assume you have watched some of what is going on in Mieza?" Apollo said.

"We have," Zeus said, putting on a fatherly smile and leaning forward. He knew Apollo was frustrated.

"I have come here as a last resort," Apollo admitted. "No matter what I do, Daphne shows no interest. I have been careful in my approach and the role I assumed. Marsyus is enthusiastic about the same things as Perseus. Marsyus does not want to possess anyone—Daphne's greatest fear."

Apollo gave Zeus a distressed look, but his father gestured for him to continue.

"Perseus's curiosity is starting to embrace the uncertainties of human life, and so trying to appreciate the journey more fully. It is a natural evolution."

Hera was pleasantly surprised. Apollo understood Daphne the way she'd hoped he would.

"Only Marsyus can complement that journey. Who else is as thoughtful?" Apollo asked.

"Yes, and as strangely witty," Hera said, smiling. "For some reason, that seems to matter to mortals."

Apollo smirked and looked up. Hera then looked at Zeus. She suspected that the only way out of Apollo's predicament would somehow involve Eros, but she did not want that.

"You chose wisely, I agree," Zeus responded. "Daphne should like you."

"And I have treaded carefully," Apollo repeated. "I made sure not to force things."

Apollo was desperate. Zeus felt it. It made him sad—truly sad, the way a father is when his child is miserable.

Zeus thought for a while and concluded that the best thing for Apollo to do was to move on. "Apollo, unfortunately, Daphne just does not seek you out. You have to make peace with that. You have gotten over many other love affairs. You will get over this one." The arrows could not be beaten.

"I have to be with her," Apollo said. "I feel so inadequate, so incomplete without her. I want to experience life, and I want to do it with her. I have not gotten over it and won't."

"You know love affairs come and go. They are disturbed easily," Zeus said emphatically.

"You must give her up," Hera said to support Zeus.

"Why? I won't. She is the one," Apollo said, getting agitated. He was convinced that his level of desperation alone warranted his father's help. Zeus didn't need to help just because Apollo wanted it, but Apollo had no other way to appeal to him. "Why can't you help?" Apollo repeated.

Zeus wanted to help. Above all else he wanted a relationship with his son. Zeus had used his powers in the past to forge relationships that were hollow—even his marriage with Hera resembled that. If he had allowed a mutual courting, without using his powers, he might have gotten the reassurance of being appreciated. This was what he now wanted from his son—appreciation, unforced appreciation. And there was no better way to gain it than to aid in the back and forth of him being a mortal. Apollo's desperate eyes demanded help like an innocent child.

"Get me Eros," Zeus yelled.

"Don't!" Hera insisted, but it was too late.

Zeus had met with Eros a few days earlier, after trying to avoid him for a while. It was a short meeting during which Eros managed to distract Zeus so much that Zeus had not learned a lot.

Zeus summoned Eros now to confirm that there was nothing that could be done.

Apollo looked offended. "That pedantic fiend? I don't want him shooting his arrows. I want genuine love, not the random kind he produces. Name one situation in which he has helped. His arrows always cause problems."

Eros arrived in time to overhear the last part of what Apollo said.

"They like it!" Eros declared. "That feeling of being suspended in midair, away from usual existence—they like it. They like the inexplicable warm fuzzy feeling. They try to explain it with physical attraction, common experiences—or my favorite: soul mates." He scoffed.

Then Eros shifted his tone. "Did you ever think that not understanding makes them worship us more?" Eros laughed with the cackle despised by all the other gods.

Apollo did not want to respond. He gave Zeus a despondent look. "Why is he here?"

"He caused the problem," Zeus said, plainly gesturing at Eros. "He should answer to you."

Eros turned as if to leave. This would not end well.

"Eros shot Daphne with a lead arrow," Zeus said.

Eros turned back and looked at Apollo. He could not resist a peek at Apollo's reaction, even if it meant he did not get away.

Hera gasped. She gave Zeus a furious look. "Here we go," she said.

"You did what?" Apollo asked, glaring at Eros.

"Just a little prick to make things interesting," Eros winced.

"*You* are a little prick, I can't believe—" Apollo started to dig into Eros. He was not only infuriated about what Eros had done in the first place, but also that Eros had encouraged him to pursue Daphne again when she was liberated from the tree.

"Stop," Zeus shouted. "Stop!" He rose from his throne.

Zeus looked at Eros. Eros was random and relished disrupting the order of things. Zeus loathed him for that and for what he had done to Apollo and Daphne. However, Zeus knew that Eros also made life more interesting. The very life Zeus enjoyed watching and occasionally participating in.

Zeus started pacing, came to the fire with the raised rim and even looked at it. *Eros is a little like Prometheus*, he thought, *difficult to control and mischievous, but he adds life.*

He looked back at Hera, who was visibly upset. She gave Zeus the same look Apollo had. She hated Eros unequivocally.

Then he looked at Apollo, whose desperation had turned to rage. Zeus knew that Apollo was thinking the least he could do was to side with him on this.

"Leave us, leave us," Zeus finally said, waving Eros away. Summoning Eros had been a mistake. He went back to his throne while Eros hastily made his getaway.

Eros was happy not to have been asked what he could do to help. He'd successfully avoided answering that question when Zeus had come to see him before. Eros had an idea, but it was not perfect, and he did not want to share it.

"I don't believe it. Are you sure he shot Daphne?" Apollo said. "Daphne liked my poem. She cried. She is yearning for a relationship. She does not appear to be robbed of emotions."

"Yes, but you forget that arrows are in regard to an individual, not everyone. She can have feelings, just not for you," Zeus explained. "She will interpret things the wrong way only in regard to you. That is what the lead arrow does."

Zeus did not have the heart to tell Apollo he had also been shot by an arrow, which was just as much the cause for his predicament. That would have made him feel that his love, or at least the beginning of it, was not real, not from within. It would not be the love Apollo saw himself as having for Daphne.

As Zeus spoke about arrows only affecting a person's feelings for one individual, Hera wondered whether Daphne's recent yearning for a relationship might lead her to someone else.

Apollo then spent some time catching up with Zeus and Hera. They avoided the hopeless topic of Daphne, and Zeus tried to build a bond with Apollo.

When Apollo finally left, Zeus resolved to speak to Eros again. This time he would keep his wits and insist they think about a solution for his son—any possible solution.

5. Daphne

Marsyus returned to Mieza on another beautiful summer day. All of Mieza would be busy, working or enjoying life, but Perseus felt like spending the day at home. It felt strange to be inside on such a day.

"I have a lot to think about," Perseus said to Phaenon when he came to Perseus's room so they could walk to class together. Kallos had already left.

Phaenon furrowed his brow. "It is not like you to stay away from lectures. Do you really want to miss out on Aristoteles's grand tour?" He walked over to the windows in the room. "Do you want me to at least open the shutters?"

"No, thank you," Perseus said quietly.

"Are you sure you're not coming?" Phaenon continued, but Perseus could not be persuaded. "Okay, then. I can make up an excuse for you, if you like." He headed for the door.

"Wait," Perseus said. "How is it going with Leviat?" Perseus asked, genuinely curious

"We are not seeing each other anymore," Phaenon said.

"Oh!" Perseus was shocked. "What happened?"

Phaenon shrugged. "She did not come to visit. I think it was her turn."

"Surely, you could have gone to see her?"

"Yes, but I think she lost interest and I am not sure I care."

It was a typical way for Phaenon to end a relationship—without much thought. If things were not perfect, he just called it off, without figuring out what was wrong. It was easy to do when things did not run deep. And ending the relationship had released him from the nagging guilt about that night with the musician. It was a relief to be done with it.

Phaenon smiled and left for the nymphaeum before Perseus could ask any further questions.

Perseus slumped. This life in Mieza was not working out right. There was so much Aristoteles did not know, Perseus felt. So much humans could only guess at. The struggle of figuring out this godly knowledge, as Aristoteles called it, was not that interesting anymore. As a child of a river god, Perseus could just return to the gods and have more knowledge. No guessing. Perfect certainty about many things.

But that was not what Perseus wanted to do, either.

The gods, with all their knowledge, just sat in their perfect temples and watched and envied humans. Their sagas were extreme tragedies or acts of heroism—immediately resolved with decisive acts. They lived in extremes. They lacked the subtleties and complexities, the love and anxieties that made human life so interesting.

Zeus and Hera heard Perseus's thoughts, but said nothing, only exchanged a distraught look. Ordinarily, Zeus would have punished such blasphemy, but he realized that Perseus was right.

"Of course, the gods don't have my feeling of inadequacy," Perseus said out loud, wondering whether being a human was worth it. "They get to retreat into their all-powerful roles."

Perseus sighed heavily.

"Love, the one thing the gods envy humans for, I don't have. The one thing that makes the vulnerabilities worthwhile.

Gods seduce humans to seek intimacy, because intimacy works best with someone who is vulnerable."

Perseus was starting to get angry. *Why am I not able to find someone I care about? Why am I burdened with all the uncertainties and shortcomings of being human, and yet denied the one advantage?*

"Perseus is miserable," Zeus said to Hera, watching this. "We need to figure something out."

"Why would concern yourself with Perseus? You know Apollo can't be the solution," Hera said.

"What if Apollo is the only one for Daphne? What if Daphne is not meant to love anyone else?" Zeus asked.

"Then that is how it is," Hera said sternly. She was not going to condone interference.

Zeus lowered his head and supported it with his hands as he sighed.

Marsyus was concerned when Perseus did not come to the lecture. He and Perseus were the most enthusiastic students. After the lecture, he went to the farmhouse.

Argo slowly led him to Perseus's room. "Perseus is not happy." Argo said sadly. "Maybe you can do something?"

It was genuine concern. Argo had come to appreciate Perseus's unassuming manner and constant attempts to see joy in things. He was not that way, but admired it in Perseus. It saddened him to see Perseus so depressed.

"I heard you were not doing well," Marsyus said as he entered Perseus's room. Perseus was dressed and sitting on the edge of the bed, and did not appear to be physically ill.

The room was a complete mess. The bed was unmade. Papers lay on the floor in the corner of the room as though they had been thrown there. A wilted plant stood on a table. Next to that Marsyus noticed the wooden box Aristoteles must have given Perseus after the Pandora lecture. Its lid was closed and scratched, and it stood askew like seemingly everything in the room.

"I just need some time," Perseus said.

Before Perseus could stop him, Marsyus walked over to the window and opened the shutters to let in some fresh air.

Below the window, Marsyus noticed planters with beautiful flowers, a little dry from not being watered but still beautiful. They had been chosen carefully and arranged to complement each other. The colors alone evoked joy. Marsyus knew better than to point them out in such a glum moment—too much of a contrast.

"What is this about?" Marsyus asked instead.

"To be honest, I feel a little like the statue in your poem. Something is missing," Perseus admitted and regretted it. It was not good to share such personal feelings, particularly when they were depressing.

"We all do," Marsyus said to Perseus. "None of us is perfect. That is what makes life interesting."

Perseus looked up at Marsyus and smiled, appreciating the sentiment, but said nothing.

"We all feel inadequate—something is always missing. As humans we have to accept that."

"I don't want perfection," Perseus said.

Good! It is hard to be intimate with perfection, Marsyus thought.

"To be honest, I don't know what I want. I look at Phaenon, who has a career and, at least for a while, he had Leviat. Don't you yearn for something like that?" Perseus said.

Marsyus scoffed. "Phaenon is incapable of having a relationship. We are better friends than he ever was with Leviat."

Marsyus was probably right, but still . . . "It would be nice to have someone," Perseus said.

Marsyus was unsure how to handle the situation. He was tempted to expose himself as Apollo, to share what he had learned from Zeus about the lead arrow, but he was not sure Perseus was ready for that. Plus, it would anger Zeus and Hera, and Marsyus was not sure what they would do.

"Give it time. You will find someone," Marsyus finally said.

Then Marsyus opened his eyes wide to produce a confident, endearing smile while looking at Perseus. He wanted to force Perseus' face to replicate his positivity. It was a little like when he'd first met Daphne, but this time instead of trying to meld their eyes, he was trying to coerce a smile by smiling. It often worked—but not this time.

"Maybe it is for the better," Perseus said despondently. "Relationships are complicated. Maybe it is best to be free like Krasi. Maybe I should count myself lucky." Perseus's face sank further. The usually joyous round face dropped its delicate lines into a mass of nothingness that shocked Marsyus. He had never seen Perseus this resigned.

"I don't agree with that at all," Marsyus said trying not to look at Perseus. He wanted to be empathetic but could not condone such negativity. "We need relationships to face an uncertain world." Marsyus looked at the flower pots in the window. "I know you don't want to be like Krasi. All he does is chase girls."

Perseus couldn't help a small chuckle at that.

"When we discussed Pygmalion's statue in class, you agreed that relationships are worthwhile," Marsyus said. Of course, Perseus had not really said that, but it was implied. "And the best ones are exclusive, worth the constraints they impose," Marsyus continued. It came out wrong and at the wrong time.

Perseus shifted uncomfortably. Exclusivity and constraints were strange topics for Marsyus to raise, and Perseus had already been too open for what felt comfortable. How could shy Marsyus have had the experience to know about such matters?

"Oh, I suppose you know about this?" Perseus said, hoping to create some distance.

At the same time, however, Perseus could not help but be intrigued. The story of Psyche had persuaded Perseus that constraints, commitment, and exclusivity were important. But such thoughts were not appropriate to share, particularly with someone as awkward as Marsyus. Perseus decided to ask a question instead.

"Why do you suppose relationships require constraints?"

"Because when you pay for it, it is worth more," Marsyus said crudely and smiled.

Marsyus saw an exclusive relationship as the ultimate compliment. When someone is willing to make a relationship exclusive, they are showing appreciation. Marysus was convinced that the gods sought relationships with humans precisely because they desired that appreciation.

"I'm serious, why?" Perseus asked again.

Marsyus knew better than to share his thoughts. It was too early, and would have scared Perseus. "You are right, I don't know what I'm talking about. Maybe it has something to do with wanting to be intimate with someone you trust." That was all he dared to say.

Perseus was surprised that they had come to similar conclusions. *Where does Marsyus get these insights?* "Interesting," was all Perseus said.

Marsyus saw the chance to push a little further. "Interesting as in that can't be true, or as in I can't believe you believe that?" Marsyus asked with a cheeky smile.

"Neither," Perseus responded, returning Marsyus's broad smile.

Then they both laughed.

Perseus was in a better place, and Marsyus knew to leave on a high note. "We all struggle," Marsyus said reassuringly as he headed for the door. He looked back at Perseus and was glad to see an expression of joy.

"I hope you come to class tomorrow. We need you," Marsyus said. "And water your plants."

6. Compromising Beauty

The day of doing nothing was lonely—lonelier than the reason Perseus had stayed away from class in the first place. If there were no prospects for a special relationship, ordinary ones were better than none, Perseus thought.

Perseus was the first to arrive at the nymphaeum the next morning. The place still felt special with its serenity and temple-like smell of candles, new wood, and must. Perseus was happy to be back in the middle of things.

As the other students arrived, they greeted Perseus warmly, but made no mention of the absence the day before. It had only been one day, and they all had difficult days in their past.

Marsyus smiled at Perseus as he came in and sat down. He did not say he was glad Perseus was back; it did not need to be said.

Aristoteles and Theophrastus also smiled at Perseus when they entered.

"Today's lecture will be in two parts." Aristoteles started with a twinkle in his eye. "It will be a beautiful compromise of nature and philosophy."

"I will first discuss the flower narcissus," Theophrastus said, "and then Aristoteles will ask you about Persephone."

Theophrastus took a deep breath and started. "What is interesting about the narcissus flower is that it grows from a bulb that is completely submerged. At the beginning of spring every year, the bulb slowly pushes a green stem about one foot tall above the ground, and then produces a yellow or white flower with six petals. The flower has a central corona that is often in a different shade of yellow and looks a little like a trumpet. The flower grows facing the sun, but unlike the sunflower does not follow the sun during the day."

"Is the flower useful for anything?" Alexander asked impatiently.

"We have done some experiments, and the flower has a strange intoxicating fragrance. I am told its name comes from the Greek word *narke*, meaning numbness, because of its heady scent. What we also discovered is that animals like rabbits and deer are somehow repelled by it. But to answer your question, no. We have not found any useful purpose for it yet, though I am hopeful. I am sure we can find a purpose for a flower with such strong properties."

"The flower even has a useless part," Marsyus said even though he was not called on. "A useless part, imagine that," Marsyus repeated. He was about as frustrated with narcissus as anyone can get with a flower. He had tried hard to find a medicinal value but could not.

"That is correct," Theophrastus responded. "Flowers are comprised of sepals, petals, stamens and pistils, each serving a distinct purpose. We are not sure why narcissus has the added element of the central corona—the trumpet. It is unusual."

Theophrastus looked at all of the students, but Marsyus in particular. "The trumpet is beautiful," he said. "It is possible that is enough?"

Theophrastus took another deep breath and continued, with his deep voice resonating over the class. "Is it possible that something that serves no function but to arouse a sense of beauty is worthwhile? Maybe it even is the most worthwhile of all things—to be able to produce an appreciation without a rational purpose. The flower unapologetically demands appreciation solely for its beauty. I believe we should give it."

The class debated this for a while. As they did, they decided that it was preferable to have a variety of purposes. However, sometimes the purity of something uncompromisingly beautiful should be appreciated. Sometimes one could appreciate something for what it was and not ask more of it, especially when the quality was as difficult to define as beauty.

Then Aristoteles started his part of the lecture. "Now, you know that Persephone appreciated narcissus," Aristoteles said, and called on Perseus to recite the story.

Perseus stood up. "Persephone was the daughter of Demeter, the goddess of nature. Hades, the god of the underworld, fell in love with Persephone and decided to kidnap her with the help of Zeus, his brother. One morning, Demeter descended to earth with Persephone and left her to play with the sea nymphs, the Nereids, and the freshwater lake nymphs, the Naiads. Demeter went to look at her bountiful crops while Persephone became interested in a beautiful valley full of . . ." Perseus paused playfully and let the class finish.

"Narcissus!" they all called out.

Perseus smiled and then continued, "The Nereids and Naiads could not leave the side of water, so Persephone went to see the narcissus by herself. They had been planted by Gaia, at the request of Zeus. Persephone pulled out one of the narcissus, and the hole that was created grew wide. Persephone froze as she heard Hades approach with horses out of the hole. The Naiad Cayne was the only one close by, and Cayne tried to rescue the crying Persephone as Hades tried to take her to the underworld. Cayne was no match for Hades. As Persephone was taken away,

Cayne melted into a pool of tears, which created a river at the spot he lost out to Hades—the very river we now call the Cayne."

"Not the way to go, Hades," Marsyus said softly.

Perseus looked down at him for a second, but then went on. "When Demeter arrived at the spot, she saw only the river and none of the Nereids or Naiads that were left could tell her what happened. She cursed them and turned them into heinous women called the sirens. Cayne, the river, at least helped by washing up Persephone's belt, indicating that something gravely wrong had occurred. Demeter got extremely upset and hunted for her daughter everywhere. She roamed earth for nine long days and nights. She met Hekate, the god of magic and witchcraft, who told her to ask Helios, the sun god. Helios finally told Demeter what happened."

Perseus paused, looked down at Marsyus, and then smiled at the class, looking forward to telling the ending. "Demeter then descended into the underworld and begged Hades to return Persephone. It was an elaborate pursuit the gods seemed to respect. Hades consulted with Zeus, and they decided to allow Persephone to live on earth for eight months each year and in the underworld for four months. Persephone ate pomegranate seeds, the fruits of her captor, which doomed her to return to the underworld again and again."

"That is beautifully told, Perseus," Aristoteles said. "A bit longer than I anticipated, but thank you. So, you know I will ask: What does this tell us? Aristoteles continued.

"How the seasons are created," Kallos said. "Eight months of spring, summer, and fall when Persephone is with mother earth, and four months of winter when she is in the underworld."

Kallos knew by now that a simple answer was probably not enough, so he added, "It is interesting that Persephone was so attracted by the narcissus's beauty that she would pull all of it out, including its fat bulb, leaving a hole that sets all the events into motion. And that narcissus now appears at the beginning of spring."

Kallos was enthusiastic, Aristoteles had to admit. "I agree that is interesting, and narcissus's beauty, bulb, and appearance in spring make it a convenient flower for the story," Aristoteles said and looked at the class. "Anything else?"

Perseus said, "It also shows that the gods are willing to interfere, first to help Hades and then to help Demeter. There is goodness in that."

"That is a broad abstraction, but true." Aristoteles said.

"The gods always interfere," Marsyus said, "but not necessarily for the better. They like playing with us, at least some of them." Marsyus folded his arms in disgust.

"That is not what I meant," Perseus said, wondering why Marsyus was so uncharacteristically upset. "They are willing to interfere for Hades, but also to correct their actions."

"You mean it shows the gods are fallible?" Marsyus asked, knowing that was not what Perseus meant, but wanting to vocalize the question for all to hear.

"No, I mean it shows that they are willing to correct their ways," Perseus said.

Marsyus fell silent. At that moment, he thought that might be the solution to his predicament. *Of course*, he thought. Zeus could do the same for him.

But then Marsyus realized that Zeus had not really corrected Hades's deed. "They didn't correct their ways. Persephone still had to spend time with Hades."

"How could they correct their actions?" Perseus responded. "They would have contradicted one of their own, either Hades or Demeter. They had to fashion a compromise."

"A compromise," Marsyus said pensively. He started thinking about what compromise he could ask Zeus for but could not come up with one.

"Yes, and Persephone accepted it. She ate the pomegranate seeds," Theophrastus said, also wondering why Marsyus was so upset.

Theophrastus said sadly, "Persephone picked beauty and ended up with a compromise." He thought that would end the lecture.

But Marsyus added, "Or Hades applied force and ended up with failure."

7. A Solution

The very next chance he got, Marsyus went to Mt. Olympus to appeal to Zeus. When he arrived, he noticed for the first time how white the temple really was. "They even made sure there are no black veins inside the white marble," he thought. Everything was stark and perfectly white. Apollo walked by the hidden flame without looking at it, and approached Zeus and Hera in their perfectly white robes. He felt intimidated, doubtful that he could persuade Zeus.

Nothing ever changes here, Apollo thought. *They just sit here in their perfect place and enforce absolute rules.*

However, as he stood in front of Zeus and Hera, Apollo steeled himself to pursuing his objective. He put on a smile and demanded they intervene the way they had for Persephone. Zeus did not even take time to contemplate what Apollo said. He gave an immediate answer; they had discussed it before Apollo arrived.

"I can't intervene," Zeus said. "What is done is done."

Hera nodded as Zeus shifted in his throne uncomfortably. He hated to cause his son so much suffering.

Hera felt it was unfortunate but necessary. "You will grow tired of Daphne, or worse, she will at the end grow tired of you. Remember Cyrene.".

Cyrene was a mortal and the queen of Cyrene, a city named after her in Africa. Apollo had loved her and had two sons with her, Aristaeus and Idmon. But Cyrene had fallen in love with Ares, Apollo's brother, and left him for several months. When she returned, she gave birth to Diomedes, Ares's son. Apollo was so enraged that he turned Cyrene into a Naiad.

Hera hoped recalling this unpleasant episode would persuade Apollo.

"And don't forget Marpessa," Zeus added, following Hera's approach. "She fell in love with Idas. I had to intervene when you confronted Idas and wanted to kill him, remember? When I finally asked Marpessa to choose between the two of you, she chose Idas."

"She was afraid I would leave her when she grew old, which was not true," Apollo responded indignantly.

"Doesn't matter. Admit it, you lost interest in her," Zeus said.

Hera was having fun now. "Do you even remember Clytie? You stopped loving her when you fell in love with Leucothoe. Clytie starved herself until she turned into a sunflower. She still moves her head all day to follow her beloved Apollo riding the chariot with the sun."

Apollo said nothing.

"Relationships are frail," Hera said. "They come and go. You will find someone else."

Zeus was curious to know what Apollo would say. He had certainly never been dissuaded from pursuing women, even for short-lived relationships.

"Daphne is different," Apollo said. "You see how she resisted Kallos, Krasi, and Phaenon. She won't leave me for someone else, and she is the one for me. I tried to explain it to you before, but I can't. To explain it is to belittle it. If I could explain it, it would probably not be true."

Zeus looked distraught and ready to help Apollo.

Hera threw up her hands. "Think of what it would mean if we reversed an act like this!" She turned to Zeus, afraid she was fighting a losing battle. "No one respects gods who admit mistakes. We are meant to be infallible. We set the rules and defend them. Who will respect our decisions if we change them?"

Hera straightened in her throne as she said this. Zeus was still slumped, agonizing over the situation.

"You intervened for Persephone and Hades," Apollo insisted.

"As gods, we are not meant to intervene," Hera insisted again.

"Exactly, humans are meant to have free will without our intervention, and that is exactly what needs to be corrected here." Apollo said, and Hera looked startled. Apollo could not help but smile a little when he realized that he could beat Hera with her own argument. "Humans are meant to have free will to act within your theoretical constraints, but the lead arrow robbed Daphne of that. She cannot be denied the quintessential quality of being human. For all the suffering that comes with it, she must be given free will within the confines *you* set."

Hera remained silent.

"When Eros determined whom Daphne cannot love, he defied the rules and became like Creon. You now have to become Antigone," Apollo begged Hera, who sat back in her throne, trying to come up with a reply.

"No one will object if you fashion a Persephone-like compromise here, except for Eros." Apollo continued.

"I spoke to him," Zeus said.

"Don't," Hera said to Zeus in one last attempt. "All this meddling is no good. It cheapens us. Don't."

Zeus could not help himself. Apollo was his son. He wanted to help. He was tired of keeping him at bay because he was illegitimate.

"There are only two things Eros can do," Zeus said reluctantly. "You must consider this carefully. He can shoot you with a lead arrow, or he can shoot Daphne with a golden arrow."

"And what would that do?" Apollo asked eagerly, before Zeus could even finish.

"It has never been done, so Eros is not sure, but if you are shot with a lead arrow, it could lessen your love for Daphne—it won't eliminate it, but it could dull it. Your torment could be less."

"And if Daphne is shot with a golden arrow?" Apollo asked.

"Well, Daphne could develop some affection for you, but nothing equal to the affection you have for her."

"In either case you will always love her more," Hera added. "So why bother?"

"Yes, that is true," Zeus said.

Apollo looked thoughtful. "So it's a question of numbing me, or creating a shared but unequal love."

"That is the best that we can do," Zeus said.

At least Apollo had choices. Difficult choices, but potential improvements over his current state. He told Zeus and Hera that he would return in three days with his decision.

8. Experiences

On his way back to Mieza, Apollo thought about what Zeus and Hera had said. They were not wrong. Apollo had had many relationships and knew all too well how fragile and terrible they could be. He started reminiscing about some of them.

Coronis was another love of his who'd fallen in love with someone else, Ischys. A crow told Apollo about the affair. When he did not believe it, he turned the crow's white feathers black. When it was finally confirmed, Apollo's sister, Artemis, killed Coronis with an arrow.

Apollo at least saved the unborn child Coronis was carrying, Asclepius. Apollo was proud of Asclepius, even though he was not his son. Asclepius became such a good doctor that Zeus became afraid he would cure all men's illnesses and killed him with a thunderbolt.

At least I avenged that, Apollo thought. Apollo had Zeus's manufacturer of thunderbolts killed. Apollo wished he could forget about it.

He still agonized over how much he loved Coronis. "It really hurts when you love someone who does not love you," he concluded.

"Then there was Hyacinth," Apollo said out loud. He tried to relax. Hyacinth he liked musing about, though it always made him sad as well.

Hyacinth was a Spartan prince who was extraordinarily handsome. Hyacinth was also admired by Zephyrs, god of the west wind, and Boreas, god of the north wind. When Apollo and Hyacinth were throwing a discus, Zephyrs, being jealous, diverted the discus by blowing on it. The discus hit Hyacinth in the head and killed him. Apollo dreaded Hyacinth's death so much that he asked to become mortal so he could die and join Hyacinth in the afterlife.

"Hera precluded that," Apollo recalled, becoming more dejected about his affairs again.

Apollo had taught Hyacinth how to play the lyre. Lyre music to this day reminded Apollo of Hyacinth, which was why he had not enjoyed the lyre music at Alexander's first party. Apollo had even created a flower in his honor, but it hurt him too much to look at it.

"Hyacinth was the closest I got to a relationship that I did not mind having even though it ended in tragedy—except for Daphne, of course."

Then there was Casandra. "At least that was not as tragic," Apollo thought.

Cassandra was the daughter of the Trojan King Priam. Apollo had tried to seduce her by bestowing the gift of prophecy on her. Cassandra, however, refused Apollo's proposition. She did not love him. Because gods were not allowed to take back their gifts, Apollo instead stripped Cassandra of her power of persuasion. Cassandra lived out her life foretelling the future with no one believing her. Apollo felt that Cassandra had gotten what she deserved. "She should have never accepted my gift," he said out loud.

But thinking about Casandra's rejection gave him pause. It was exactly the type of rejection he might continue to face with Daphne.

There had even been another love affair that ended in a lover turning into a tree, like Daphne. Cyparrissus was the son of Telephus, a descendant of the demigod Hercules. That love affair had come to an end when Cyparrissus mistakenly killed the pet deer Apollo gave him. Cyparrissus was filled with such grief over the loss that he turned himself into a Cypress tree.

So many love affairs and none ended well, Apollo thought, discouraged. His face looked like Perseus's had the day Perseus stayed away from the lecture—distorted, empty, and yearning for the seemingly unattainable.

"Daphne is special. She was my first love." He argued with himself to see if he could persuade himself that it was worth it to continue the pursuit. *No one gets over their first love affair*, Apollo thought, though he was not sure it was true.

Apollo thought about his options. He had a chance to continue the affair, but it would not be what he intended it to be. He loved Daphne, but could he live a life where the love she returned was always weaker? In such a case, would it not be better to live a life where his own love was dulled? Would it not be better to be able to live life without the struggle Daphne would bring—the constant struggle of wanting more? Was he setting himself up for a constant torment that might only end like all his other love affairs—in tragedy?

9. A Private Lesson

When Apollo was back in Mieza as Marsyus, he could not help but obsess about the decision he had to make. It was wearing him out. He tried to distract himself by working with Theophrastus.

They gathered in the main room of the house, the one that had plants throughout, with the ones being analyzed sitting on tables, while others rested on the floor. Theophrastus was standing in front of one of those tables working on an aloe vera plant. His fingers and clothes were already dirty. He even had dirt on his face where he had wiped off sweat.

Theophrastus and Marsyus were working on spontaneous reproduction, the concept Aristoteles had mentioned in class. They noticed that aloe vera plants grew little offsets at their base but also flowered. They had carefully cut off any flowers that grew on some aloe vera plants months ago to test whether the plants could reproduce without them.

"The plants whose flowers we cut off still reproduced through the offsets," Theophrastus declared victoriously. "They spontaneously reproduce."

"So aloe veras have unnecessary extra capabilities. They can reproduce with flowers and spontaneously with offsets. Another plant with unnecessary parts," Marsyus said instead of cheering.

"Yes, except maybe it is a beneficial form of redundancy. There could be a purpose to both," Theophrastus retorted.

"You really believe that aloe veras are so well planned out?" Marsyus said angrily. "Surely the gods would not bother with duplication. They would not intervene with such detail and care.”

“Don’t say that. Demeter gave us such diversity of flowers,” Theophrastus said. “What a strange thing for you to say.” He wondered what could be upsetting the boy.

Theophrastus and Marsyus had become close during their time in Mieza. Theophrastus had even shared that his real name was Tyrtamus. Back in Athens, Aristoteles had started to call him Theophrastus, since he thought Theophrastus had a god-like way of speaking. *Theo* for god and *phrastus* for phrasing, he told him. “An accolade I don’t deserve,” Theophrastus insisted.

“What has gotten into you lately?” Theophrastus asked gently.

Marsyus did not answer and instead decided to ask Theophrastus for advice. “Can I ask you about Apollo and Daphne?” Marsyus asked. It was a strange thing to ask. Theophrastus took it as a deflection.

“Of course. A tragic story.” Theophrastus would humor him. “But shouldn’t you ask Aristoteles about such matters?”

“Have you ever thought, what if Apollo had a second chance? What if he could choose between lessening his love for Daphne and having Daphne love him a little?” Marsyus asked. “Not as a tree, I mean.”

Theophrastus could not resist but to ponder it. “Less love or more love, an interesting hypothetical. I suppose he should opt for more love,” he finally said, “though I am not sure.”

“You would rather have more of Demeter’s flowers,” Marsyus said with a smile. “More of a good thing.”

"I suppose, but I will take the ugly ones as well."
Theophrastus chuckled and held up an aloe vera plant.
Theophrastus was happy that Marsyus seemed in a better place.

"Speaking of aloe veras, I tested their fleshy leaves,"
Marsyus said. "The liquid in them seems to soothe the pain of
sunburn." Marsyus had tested it on himself several times. "But I
have not found any other benefits."

"Not even for other wounds, like cuts?" Theophrastus
asked.

"There were no other wounds to test it on. The only
wounds anyone gets around here are emotional," Marsyus said—
now joking, which pleased Theophrastus.

Marsyus thought about Hephaestion and Kallos's fight.
Even that hadn't resulted in any injuries—physical or emotional.
He had recently seen Kallos teach both Alexander and
Hephaestion how to race horses. Kallos seemed to have found a
way to ingratiate himself with the future king.

Marsyus returned to the discussion of aloe veras. "I
know I should have confirmed more, but I just don't think I can
prove other aspects, and I want to be cautious. I am sorry."

Theophrastus would have preferred Marsyus to be a little
more of a risk-taker, but risk-taking was something Marsyus still
needed to get used to.

"Well, it is not much, but we are bringing some order to
things," Theophrastus announced, surprisingly content.
"Aristoteles wants to see us. We can report on the offset findings
and your sunburn treatment."

When Theophrastus and Marsyus arrived at Aristoteles's house,
Aristoteles was hard at work sitting at the table on the left of his

study. Theophrastus and Marsyus sat down at the table on the right and started laying out their work, when, to everyone's surprise, Alexander appeared.

"May I come in?" Alexander asked.

Aristoteles was startled, cleared his throat, and waved Alexander in. Alexander looked around the room but did not see the Venus flytrap plant he had left. He'd intended to start his conversation with Aristoteles about it but now could not.

"What are you working on?" Alexander asked instead.

"I am pulling together some thoughts for a book I am considering writing about ethics," Aristoteles answered.

"That is interesting. What would the book be focused on? Is it a collection of your lectures?" Alexander asked.

"No, that would be a collection of questions, wouldn't it?" Aristoteles said and smiled at Theophrastus who produced a chuckle.

Then Aristoteles saw his opportunity to address an issue he had been meaning to bring up with Alexander ever since he'd met with Olympias in Pella. He'd promised her he would speak to Alexander about how he could avoid some of the excesses of his father.

"The book is mainly about temperance. You see, I believe that reasoning and emotions are often in conflict. This we discussed in class. What we did not discuss is what you do about it. I advocate that you force yourself to find the right balance between them and develop good habits of keeping that balance. This way, you can avoid the constant conflict."

Alexander nodded.

"Take the example of money," Aristoteles continued. "In taking and giving money, the middle ground is generosity, the excess is extravagance or spendthriftiness, and the deficiency is stinginess or cheapness. You have to use intellect to create the right balance of how to spend and then make that a habit that becomes natural. Once you develop that habit, the conflict abates, and you become a moral man."

Alexander enthusiastically agreed. "I have heard this for soldiers. Too much fear leads to cowardice, too much courage to foolhardiness. The best soldiers use reason to find the middle ground and fight accordingly."

"Precisely. You always want to find a balance and make that your habit. A stomach you feed too little shrinks and dies; a stomach you feed too much gets too big and needs more food. Make eating right a habit, and you avoid the struggle."

"The problem is, how do you know what is too much?" Alexander asked. "How do you know where the balance is?

"I agree, that is not always easy," Aristoteles said. "But if you seek balance, you are at least on the right path."

Aristoteles left it at that. He could not criticize the king for his excesses, but he knew Alexander would understand.

Alexander started thinking about the many fights his father had with his mother. The tension his debauched desires caused. He never wanted to be in a situation like that. He vowed to develop habits that would not lead to that.

Marsyus listened to the conversation. He pretended to be working, but he hung on every word. "Seek a balance" and "habits that take away the struggle" reverberated in his mind. Marsyus had assumed that love, of all emotions, should be absolute. In the stories of the gods, love was an extreme. Yet the balance Aristoteles had outlined applied to his situation.

You can live with tempered emotions, Marysus thought. *Maybe as a human, you have to, no matter what?* It was an important realization for him.

Alexander turned to Aristoteles. "So, where is the plant I left for you?"

"We fed it to Pan," Theophrastus joked. "They belong to each other—grotesque plants, animals, humans or whatever they are."

Aristoteles did not want to make light of Alexander's question. He knew Alexander had developed a genuine interest in plants. "Marsyus and Theophrastus told me it had to be you," he said. "You were right to bring it here. Marsyus told me it fascinated you. The plant certainly astonished me. It makes our project harder. Here we have a plant that reaches over into the animal kingdom, but I am still not convinced it can sense things the way animals can."

"So what will you do?" Alexander asked.

"For the time being, we've decided to ignore it. We have put it away. We refuse to stop what we are doing because of it. Eventually, though, we may all have to accept that not all things are as black and white as we would like them to be."

10. Daphne Emerges

Apollo took every last hour of his remaining time after that to consider his decision.

His many love affairs led him in one direction, but what he'd learned in Mieza led him in another. There were so many disappointing entanglements, so many tragedies caused by inadequacies that could not have been foretold but should have been avoided. Then, there was the inexplicable desire to participate in those inadequacies, to live in them and appreciate the uncertainties they bring. Ambiguities to revel in.

On the third day, Apollo returned to Mount Olympus.

He wore a broad smile, not so much because he was happy with what he was about to embark on but because he had made a decision. He was glad that part was over.

Hera was the first to react when Apollo announced his decision.

"This meddling continues to get us into trouble," Hera said. For a moment Apollo was afraid she might try again to persuade Zeus not to help. "But I am happy with the decision you made. It stands for life. You have chosen life," she repeated and smiled at him. Apollo had become the type of man she, the god of marriage, respected. A man who appreciated love and understood its limitations.

Hearing the passion with which Apollo described his decision, Hera even wished she could do something to get Zeus to be that way with her. *Maybe I could be less certain*, she thought briefly. *No, it would be ungodly. I can't.*

"I am proud of you as well, my son," Zeus said. He wanted to tell Apollo that he would have made the same choice but was afraid of upsetting Hera with such talk. If Apollo had not been his son, he would have been jealous. Jealous of the hope that Apollo brought to his relationship with Daphne.

"So it shall be done," Zeus said, happy to be able to help with something he believed in.

Apollo was relieved. All he wanted to hear from Zeus and Hera was support for his decision. He had already spent too much time trying to rationalize it.

"Will you make sure that Eros does not mess it up—like when he accidentally shot himself and fell in love with Psyche? I hate to see him do that in this case." Apollo asked Zeus upon his departure.

"I will make sure his aim is perfect," Zeus promised.

They joined eyes with shared apprehension about Eros and appreciation of restraints in relationships. Nothing could have bonded them more.

Upon returning to Mieza as Marsyus, Apollo spent time by himself, waiting for events to unfold. A calm came over him. He reveled in the reprieve of just needing to wait.

Marsyus even avoided speaking to Perseus at the lessons he attended. "In these matters, the inevitable is a mystery and a blessing, and it is best not to interfere or create any doubt," he thought.

He went on walks and picked a bouquet of narcissus to bring home to admire. "They are beautiful," he thought as he studied the yellow trumpets of the flowers. It brought a smile to his face. "Beauty for beauty's sake." Then he thought about Persephone's fate after she picked narcissus and thought still with a smile, "At least I know what I am getting into."

Three days later, a great summer storm formed on the horizon. All the students were sent home early from the nymphaeum, and asked to wait out the storm in their homes studying texts that Aristoteles had given them.

Perseus thought it might be a good opportunity to study with Marsyus, but Marsyus had left the nymphaeum as soon as they were sent home, not lingering as he usually would to discuss the matters from the lecture. Kallos left to spend time with Alexander and Hephaestion; Phaenon asked and was allowed to join them. Perseus walked back to the farmhouse alone and found it deserted.

Perseus opened the shutters to let in the little light that existed outside with the brewing storm. It was dark and barely possible to make out the flowers in the flowerpots if not for their subtle scent. Black clouds were engulfing the outside. Perseus lit a candle to study the papers Aristoteles wanted them to read, but the wind from the storm quickly blew it out. Perseus lit it again, and it blew out again. Perseus thought of closing the shutters but did not want to sit in the dark room all alone.

Instead of reading, Perseus lay down, trying to relax, with only the impending storm to smell and listen to.

The feeling of incompleteness, of wanting, that Perseus had complained to Marsyus about reappeared. Perseus was upset that it could not be shaken.

Perseus tried to cheer up by watching and listening to the storm as it kicked up with blinding lightning and roaring thunder. Perseus lay there quietly, trying to enjoy the storm like in the past—alternating between watching the lightning through the window and watching the empty shadows on the walls in the room. There was no joy in it. Perseus could not enjoy such stillness anymore. Life had to be lived. It required more.

Then Perseus tried to recount all they had learned in Mieza—the many lectures. It had started so rationally. There were a lot of good thoughts, thoughts about how societies should be organized, about morality, and about science. Yet, they learned it was not all clear-cut. There was ambiguity in everything. The world was not just rational.

Even relationships seemed tenuous and fleeting—Phaenon and Leviat's was a testament to that. Relationships seemed to have the same ambiguities as they had learned about in the lessons. Still, the idea of a good relationship was the only thing that brought a smile to Perseus's face. Perseus had fond memories of the times spent as Daphne with Apollo, in the back and forth with students in classes, at the river swimming and parties with the other students.

Perseus was particularly happy about the time Marsyus had come to the farmhouse to provide much needed friendship and encouragement. Marsyus was smart, inquisitive, kind, and gentle. "Probably the best person out of the group," Perseus said out loud.

But Marsyus was also shy and awkward. At the parties, he stood in the shadows. He did not participate. Then there were the awkward moments after the boar hunt and after the painting project. The awkward conversation they'd had during the visit to the farmhouse.

Despite all the ambiguities, Perseus was certain that what was worse than Mieza were the white sterile walls of the temple on Mount Olympus. "Perfectly pristine white walls, thrones and robes; absolute power, strict rules, and no uncertainty," Perseus scoffed. "So uninteresting that all the gods want to do is watch humans."

Perseus lay there with empty eyes, disillusioned—quiet, sad and lonely; finally falling asleep while the storm was still rumbling.

The next morning, Perseus woke up abruptly with one surprising thought: What if Marsyus' shyness should be interpreted as a strength?

Maybe Marsyus knew how superficial the parties were. That is why he stood in the shadows. Maybe Marsyus wanted to talk about the boar hunt or the painting because there were lessons in them. There was more to be learned, or he wanted the experiences to be more complete. More complete by reliving them with someone.

Why should shyness be seen as a weakness? If it is rooted in understanding how uncertain things are, if it is rooted in thoughtfulness, is it not a sign of strength? It is not awkward; it is endearing. It represents precisely what makes life so interesting.

Perseus vowed to get to know Marsyus better - to explore life to the fullest.

On the windowsill of the room above the planter filled with flowers watered by the storm stood the wooden box Perseus had asked Aristoteles for after the Pandora lecture.

It was wide open.

THE END